ISBN 1 85854 176 X
© Brimax Books Ltd 1995.
Published by Brimax Books Ltd, Newmarket, England 1995.
Printed in Spain.

# Little Women

ADAPTED BY
# JOHN ESCOTT

ILLUSTRATED BY
# GAVIN ROWE

Brimax . Newmarket . England

# Introduction

Louisa M. Alcott's *Little Women* has been a well-loved classic of literature since it was first published in 1868. It tells the story of Meg, Jo, Beth and Amy. They are four sisters who try to lead as normal a life as possible with the absence of their father and their lack of money.

During their father's absence, Mr Laurence, the girls' wealthy neighbour becomes their friend and protector. He has a special fondness for Beth, who plays the piano for him. When her husband becomes ill, Mrs March goes to nurse him and the girls are left alone. They do their best without her but the days seem very long and tiring, then poor Beth is taken ill with scarlet fever.

The beautiful illustrations along with the carefully adapted text make  this a book that every child will love to read.

# Contents

# Chapter 1

# Playing Pilgrims

"CHRISTMAS won't be Christmas without any presents," grumbled Jo, lying on the rug.

"It's so dreadful to be poor!" sighed Meg, looking at her old dress.

"It's not fair for some girls to have pretty things, and others nothing at all," added little Amy, with an injured sniff.

"We've got Father and Mother, and each other anyhow," said Beth.

The four young faces brightened in the firelight, but darkened again as Jo said sadly, "We haven't got Father, and shan't have him for a long time." She didn't say 'perhaps never', but each silently added it, thinking of Father away where the fighting was.

Then Meg said, "Mother says we ought not to spend money for pleasure when our men are suffering in the army."

"I agree not to expect anything from Mother or you," said Jo, "but Mother won't wish us to give up everything. Let's each buy ourselves what we want, and have a little fun. We work hard to earn it."

"I know I do, teaching those dreadful children all day when I'm longing to enjoy myself at home," began Meg.

"How would you like to be shut up for hours with a nervous, fussy old lady?" said Jo.

"It's naughty to complain," said Beth, "but I think washing dishes and keeping things tidy is the worst work in the world.

My hands get too stiff to practise my music." She looked at her rough hands with a sigh.

"You don't have to go to school with girls who laugh at your dresses and say cruel things because your father isn't rich," said Amy.

"Don't you wish we had the money Papa lost when we were little, Jo?" said Meg. "How happy and good we'd be if we had no worries."

Jo sat up and began to whistle.

"Don't Jo, it's so boyish," said Amy.

"I wish I *was* a boy," said Jo, "because then I could go and fight with Papa, not stay at home and knit like a poky old woman!"

"Poor Jo," said Beth. "You must try to be content with making your name boyish and playing brother to us girls."

"As for you, Amy," said Meg, "you are too prim. You'll grow up a pompous little goose if you don't take care."

"If Jo is a tomboy and Amy a goose, what am I, please?" asked Beth.

"You're a dear, and nothing else," answered Meg, warmly, and no one disagreed, for Beth was the pet of the family.

Meg was sixteen and very pretty, with large eyes and soft brown hair. Fifteen-year-old Jo was very tall and thin, with a comical nose and sharp grey eyes. Her long chestnut-coloured hair was usually bundled into a net, out of the way. Beth was thirteen,

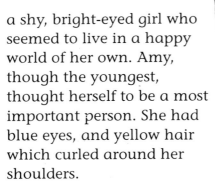

a shy, bright-eyed girl who seemed to live in a happy world of her own. Amy, though the youngest, thought herself to be a most important person. She had blue eyes, and yellow hair which curled around her shoulders.

The clock struck six. Beth put a pair of slippers down to warm, Meg lit the lamp, Amy got out of the easy-chair without being asked, and Jo forgot how tired she was and held the slippers closer to the fire.

"These are quite worn out," she said. "Marmee must have a new pair."

"I thought I'd get her some with my dollar," said Beth.

"No, I shall!" cried Amy.

"I'm the oldest – " began Meg.

But Jo cut in with, "I'm the man of the family now Papa is away, and I shall buy them."

"Let's each get her something and not get anything for ourselves," said Beth.

"That's so like you, dear!" said Jo. "What will we get?"

Everyone thought for a moment, then Meg announced, "I shall give her a nice pair of gloves."

"Army shoes, best to be had," cried Jo.

"Some handkerchiefs, all hemmed," said Beth.

"I'll get a little bottle of cologne; it won't cost much, so I'll have some money left to buy something for me," added Amy.

"We'll let Marmee think we're getting things for ourselves, and then surprise her," said Jo.

Mrs March arrived home soon after. She took off her wet things and put on her warm slippers, and the girls flew about trying to make things comfortable. Meg arranged the tea-table, Jo brought wood for the fire, Beth trotted between the parlour and the kitchen, quiet and busy, while Amy gave orders.

"I've got a treat for you," Mrs March said with a happy face.

"A letter!" cried Jo. "Three cheers for Father!"

"I think it was splendid of him to go as a chaplain when he was too old to be drafted, and not strong enough for a soldier," said Meg.

It was a cheerful letter, and the special message for the girls came at the end: *'Give them all my love and a kiss. Tell them I think of them by day and pray for them by night. I know they will be loving children to you, will do their duty faithfully, and that when I come back I will be fonder and prouder than ever of my little women.'*

Jo was not ashamed of the tear that dropped off the end of her nose, and Amy did not mind rumpling her curls as she hid her face on Mother's shoulder.

"I'm a selfish pig," she sobbed, "but I'll truly try to be better."

"We all will!" cried Meg. "I think too much of my looks and hate to work, but I won't any more."

"I'll try to be what he loves to call me, 'a little woman'," said Jo, "and not be rough and wild."

Beth said nothing, just wiped away her tears and began to knit furiously at a blue army sock which she was making.

Mrs March broke the silence that followed by saying, "Do you remember how you used to play *Pilgrim's Progress*? I used to tie bundles on your backs for burdens and you'd travel through the house from the cellar, which was the City of Destruction, up to the house-top where you had all the lovely things you could collect to make the Celestial City."

"What fun it was!" said Jo, remembering.

"If I wasn't too old for such things, I'd play it again," said Amy.

"It is a play we are playing all the time, my dear," said Mrs March. "Our burdens are here, our road is before us, and the longing for goodness and happiness is what leads us through troubles and mistakes to the peace which is a true Celestial City.

Suppose you begin again, my little pilgrims, not in play but in earnest, and see how far you can get before Father comes home."

"Really, Mother, where are our bundles?" asked Amy.

"Each of you said what your burden was a moment ago, except Beth who I rather think hasn't got any."

"Yes, I have," said Beth. "Mine is dishes and dusters, and envying girls with nice pianos, and being afraid of people."

Beth's bundle was such a funny one that everyone wanted to laugh. But nobody did, for it would have hurt her feelings.

"Let's do it," said Meg. "It's only another name for trying to be good, and the story may help us. But we ought to have our roll of directions, as in the story."

"Look under your pillows on Christmas morning," said Mrs March, "and you will find your guide-book."

That evening, needles flew as the girls made sheets for Aunt March. And for once, no one grumbled about the work. At nine o'clock they stopped to sing a song. Beth played the old piano, softly touching the yellow keys, and Meg and her mother led the little choir. Amy chirped like a cricket, and Jo always managed to come in at the wrong place, but the girls never grew too old to sing together.

# Chapter 2

# *A Merry Christmas*

JO was the first to wake in the grey dawn of Christmas morning. No stockings hung at the fireplace, and for a moment she felt disappointed. Then she remembered to look under her pillow and found a little crimson-coloured book. She woke Meg who did the same, and a green-covered book appeared with the same picture inside, and a few words written by their mother. Presently, Beth and Amy woke to find their little books – one dove-coloured, the other blue.

"Mother wants us to read and think about these books," Meg said seriously, "and we must begin at once. I shall read a little every morning when I wake, for I know it will help me through the day."

She opened her new book and began to read. Jo put an arm around her and read also, with the quiet expression so seldom seen on her face.

"Let's do as they do, Amy," said Beth. "I'll help you with the hard words and they'll explain things if we don't understand."

And then the rooms were very still while the pages were softly turned, and Winter sunshine crept in to touch the bright heads and serious faces with a Christmas greeting.

"Where is Mother?" asked Meg later, as she and Jo ran down to thank her for their gifts.

"Goodness only knows," said old Hannah. She had lived with the family since Meg was born and was considered more as a friend than a servant. "Some poor creature came a-beggin' and your ma went straight off to see what was needed."

"She'll be back soon," said Meg. She looked at the presents which were in a basket under the sofa, ready to be produced at the proper time. "Where is Amy's bottle of cologne?"

"She went to put some ribbon on it, or some such notion," said Jo.

"How nice my handkerchiefs look, don't they?" said Beth. "Hannah washed and ironed them for me, and I marked them all myself." She looked proudly at the somewhat uneven letters.

Jo laughed. "She's put 'Mother' on them instead of 'M. March'. How funny!"

"I thought it was better to do that," said Beth, looking troubled. "Meg's initials are 'M.M.' and I don't want anyone to use them but Marmee."

"It's a very pretty and sensible idea," said Meg, frowning at Jo.

"Here's Mother, hide the basket, quick!" said Jo, as a door slammed and steps sounded in the hall.

But it was Amy. She came in hastily, wearing her hood and cloak.

"Where have you been, and what are you hiding behind you?" asked Meg.

"I ran to the corner shop and changed the little bottle of cologne for a big one," said Amy. "I gave *all* my money to get it, and I'm not going to be selfish any more!"

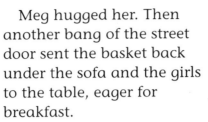

Meg hugged her. Then another bang of the street door sent the basket back under the sofa and the girls to the table, eager for breakfast.

"Merry Christmas, Marmee!" they cried. "Thank you for our books. We read some, and mean to every day."

"Merry Christmas, little daughters! I'm glad you began at once, and hope you will keep on. But I want to say a word before we sit down. Not far away lies a poor woman with a new-born baby. Six children are huddled in one bed to keep from freezing, for they have no fire. There is nothing to eat and they are hungry and cold. My girls, will you give them your breakfast as a Christmas present?"

For a minute no one spoke. Then Jo said, "I'm glad you came before we began!"

"May I help carry the things to the poor little children?" said Beth.

"*I* shall take the cream and muffins," added Amy, giving up the things she liked most.

Meg covered the buckwheats and piled bread on to one big plate.

"I thought you'd do it," said Mrs March, smiling.

It was early, so few people saw the funny procession.

A bare, miserable room it was, with no fire, ragged bed-clothes, a sick mother, a wailing baby, and a group of pale, hungry children huddled under one old quilt to keep them warm.

"The good angels have come to us!" said the poor woman, crying for joy as the girls went in.

Hannah, who had carried wood, made a fire. Mrs March gave the mother tea and gruel, then she dressed the little baby as tenderly as if it had been her own. The girls set the children round the fire and fed them like hungry birds.

It was a very happy meal, although the girls got none of it. But when they went away, there were not four merrier people than those hungry girls who gave away their breakfast on Christmas morning.

"Three cheers for Marmee!" cried Jo.

Beth played a march on the piano, Amy threw open the door, and Meg escorted their mother into the room with great dignity. Mrs March was both surprised and touched when she saw her presents and read the little notes which were with them. The slippers went on at once, a new handkerchief was slipped into her pocket, scented with Amy's cologne, and the gloves were pronounced 'a perfect fit'. Then there was a good deal of laughing and kissing and explaining.

The rest of the day was spent getting things ready for the evening when the girls were to perform a play which Jo had written. Jo would play the male parts, and took great pleasure in a pair of leather boots given to her by a friend. These boots, an old foil and a slashed doublet were her chief treasures and appeared on all occasions.

On Christmas night, a dozen girls piled on to the bed, which was the 'dress circle', and sat expectantly before the blue and yellow chintz curtains. There was a lot of whispering and an occasional giggle from behind the curtains, then a bell sounded and they flew apart.

'A gloomy wood' had been made with a few shrubs in pots and a green baize on the floor, and a cave using a clothes-horse for a roof and bureaus for walls. Inside the cave was an old witch bending over a black pot.

In came Hugo, the villain, with a sword, a black beard, a mysterious cloak – and the boots. He sang of his hatred of Roderigo, his love for Zara, and how he would kill one to win the other. Then he went to the cave and ordered Hagar to come forth.

Out came Meg, with grey horse-hair hanging about her face. Hugo demanded a potion to make Zara adore him and one to destroy Roderigo. Hagar called up the spirit to bring the love potion and a little figure appeared with glittering wings, golden hair and a garland of roses on its head. It waved a wand, sang a song, and dropped a small bottle at the witch's feet. Hagar called again and an ugly black imp appeared. It croaked a reply, tossed a dark bottle at Hugo, then disappeared with a mocking laugh. Hugo took the potions and departed, then Hagar told the audience that, because Hugo had once killed friends of hers, she had cursed him and would take her revenge.

The curtain fell and the audience ate candy while they waited.

A good deal of hammering went on before the curtain went back again. A tower rose to the ceiling, and halfway up was a window where Zara appeared in a blue and silver dress, waiting for Roderigo. He came, wearing a plumed cap and a red cloak – and the boots, of course. Kneeling at the foot of the tower with a guitar, he sang a serenade to Zara, then threw a rope ladder up and invited her to climb down. She crept from her window, put her hand on Roderigo's shoulder and was about to leap down. But she forgot her train, which caught in the window. The tower tottered, fell with a crash, and buried the lovers in the ruins!

Don Pedro, the cruel sire, rushed in and dragged out his daughter whispering, "Don't laugh, act as if it was all right!" and ordered Roderigo to leave the kingdom. But his daughter and Roderigo defied him and he sent them to the deepest dungeons of the castle.

Act Three was the castle hall, where Hagar came to free the lovers and finish Hugo. She heard him coming, hid, then saw him put the potions into two cups of wine. He told a servant to take them to the captives in their cells. The servant took Hugo aside to tell him something and Hagar changed the two cups for two others which were harmless. The servant carried them away and Hagar put back the cup which held the poison meant for Roderigo. Hugo drank it and, after a good deal of stamping and clutching, fell flat and died.

Act Four showed Roderigo about to stab himself because he'd been told Zara had deserted him. A song was sung under his window telling him Zara was true, but in danger. A key was thrown in which would unlock the door, and Roderigo tore off his chains and rushed away to rescue his lady-love.

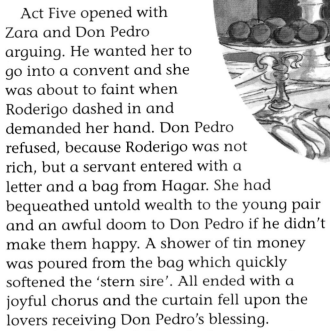

Act Five opened with Zara and Don Pedro arguing. He wanted her to go into a convent and she was about to faint when Roderigo dashed in and demanded her hand. Don Pedro refused, because Roderigo was not rich, but a servant entered with a letter and a bag from Hagar. She had bequeathed untold wealth to the young pair and an awful doom to Don Pedro if he didn't make them happy. A shower of tin money was poured from the bag which quickly softened the 'stern sire'. All ended with a joyful chorus and the curtain fell upon the lovers receiving Don Pedro's blessing.

Loud applause followed – but stopped abruptly when the 'dress circle' bed collapsed under the enthusiastic audience! Happily, no one was hurt.

Just then, Hannah appeared. "Would the young ladies like to come down to supper?" she said.

This was a surprise, even to the actors. And when they saw the table, they looked at each other in amazement. There was ice-cream, cake and fruit, and French bonbons, and in the middle of the table were four great bouquets of hot-house flowers.

"Is it fairies?" asked Amy.

"It's Santa Claus," said Beth.

"Mother did it," said Meg, through her grey beard.

"Aunt March had a good fit and sent the supper," cried Jo.

"All wrong. Old Mr Laurence sent it," replied Mrs March.

"The Laurence boy's grandfather!" exclaimed Meg. "What put such an idea into his head? We don't know him."

"Hannah told one of his servants about your breakfast party, and that pleased him. He knew my father years ago, and sent a note saying that he wanted to send my children a few trifles in honour of the day."

"That boy put it into his head, I know he did!" said Jo. "He'd like to know us, but he's shy, and Meg's so prim she won't let me speak to him."

The plates went round and the ice began to melt out of sight, with 'Ohs!' and 'Ahs!' of satisfaction.

"You mean the people who live in the big house next door, don't you?" said one of the girls. "My mother knows old Mr Laurence. She says he's proud and doesn't like to mix with his neighbours. He keeps his grandson shut up when the boy isn't riding or walking with his tutor, and makes him study very hard. We invited him to our party but he didn't come."

"That boy needs fun, I'm sure he does," said Jo.

# Chapter 3

# *The Laurence Boy*

"JO, JO! Where are you?" cried Meg, at the foot of the garret stairs.

"Here," answered a husky voice from above.

Meg found her sister sitting on an old sofa by the sunny window, eating apples and crying over a story book. It was Jo's favourite place, where she loved to sit quietly with half a dozen apples and a nice book.

"Look! An invitation from Mrs Gardiner for tomorrow night!" cried Meg, waving the paper before reading it with girlish delight. "'Mrs Gardiner would be happy to see Miss March and Miss Josephine at a little party on New Year's Eve.' Marmee says we can go, but what shall we wear?"

"Our poplins," said Jo, "because we haven't anything else."

"If only I had a silk!" sighed Meg.

"Our pops are nice enough. Yours is as good as new, but I forgot the burn and the tear in mine. The burn shows badly and I can't take it out."

"You must keep your back out of sight, the front is all right. I'll have a new ribbon for my hair, Marmee will lend me her little pearl pin, my new slippers are lovely, and my gloves will do."

"Mine are spoilt with lemonade, I'll have to go without," said Jo.

"You *must* have gloves!" cried Meg. "You can't dance without them."

"Then we'll each wear one good one and carry a bad one."

"Your hands are bigger than mine and you'll stretch my glove dreadfully!" began Meg.

"Then I'll go without, I don't care." Jo picked up her book.

"You may have it, you may! Only don't stain it, and do behave nicely. Don't put your hands behind you, or stare, or say 'Christopher Columbus!' will you?"

"Don't worry about me," said Jo. "Now go and answer your note and let me finish this story."

New Year's Eve came.

Mrs Gardiner greeted Meg and Jo and handed them over to the eldest of her six daughters. Meg knew Sallie and was quickly at her ease, but Jo stood with her back carefully against the wall and felt out of place.

The dancing began and Meg was asked at once. Jo saw a big red-headed youth coming towards her and quickly slipped into a curtained recess. Unfortunately, another bashful person had chosen the same refuge and she found herself face to face with the 'Laurence boy'.

"I didn't know anyone was here," stammered Jo.

The boy laughed. "Don't mind me," he said, "stay if you like. I only came in here because I don't know any people. I think I've seen you before. You live near us, don't you?"

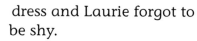

"Next door," said Jo. "We enjoyed your nice Christmas present."

"Grandpa sent it, Miss March."

"But you put the idea into his head, didn't you, Mr Laurence? And I'm not Miss March, I'm only Jo."

"And I'm not Mr Laurence, only Laurie."

"Do you like parties?" asked Jo.

"Sometimes," he said. "But I've been abroad a good many years and don't know how you do things here."

"Abroad!" cried Jo. "Oh, tell me about it!"

And he told her how he had been to school in Vevey, where the boys had a fleet of boats on the lake and went for walking trips about Switzerland with their teachers.

"Did you go to Paris?" asked Jo.

"We spent last Winter there."

"Can you talk French? Do say some."

He spoke a few words and Jo listened carefully. "Let's see," she said, "you asked, 'who is the lady in the pretty slippers?' It's my sister, Meg, which you knew! Do you think she's pretty?"

"Yes. She looks so fresh and quiet, and dances like a lady."

Jo glowed with pleasure at this boyish praise of her sister, and stored it up to repeat to Meg. They both chatted until they felt like old friends and Jo soon forgot her

dress and Laurie forgot to be shy.

"Are you going to college soon?" she asked him.

"Not for two or three years," he said. "I won't go until I'm seventeen, anyway."

He suddenly looked very serious and not altogether happy, so Jo changed the subject and said, "Why don't you go and dance?"

"If you will come too," he answered.

"I can't because – " Jo stopped, not sure whether to tell or laugh.

"Because what?"

"You won't tell?"

"Never!"

"Well, I've a bad trick of standing before the fire, and I burn my frocks. I scorched this one and though it's mended, it shows. Meg told me to keep still so that no one would see it. You can laugh if you like."

But Laurie didn't laugh. Instead, he said gently, "Never mind that. Please come."

Jo thanked him and gladly went, wishing she had two neat gloves when she saw the nice pearl-coloured ones her partner wore.

When the music stopped they sat down and began to talk, but Meg appeared and beckoned her sister. Jo followed her into a side room.

"I've sprained my ankle," said Meg, holding her foot and looking pale. "That stupid high heel turned and gave me a bad

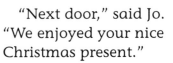

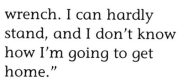

wrench. I can hardly stand, and I don't know how I'm going to get home."

"You'll have to get a carriage," said Jo.

"It will cost ever so much. I dare say I can't get one at all, for most people come in their own, and it's a long way to the stable and no one to send. I'll rest until Hannah comes, then do the best I can."

"I'll ask Laurie, he'll go," said Jo.

"No, don't ask or tell anyone! Just tell me when Hannah comes."

"They're going for supper now," said Jo. "I'll stay with you."

"No, run along and bring me some coffee," said Meg. "I'm so tired."

Jo went blundering away to the dining room, found the coffee, but immediately spilt some down the front of her dress!

"What a blunderbuss I am!" she said, wiping it with Meg's glove.

"Can I help you?" said a friendly voice. And there was Laurie with a full cup in one hand and a plate of ice in the other.

"I was trying to get something for Meg," said Jo. "She's tired."

"And I was looking for someone to give this to," he said.

"Oh, thank you. I'll show you where she is."

Laurie brought more coffee and an ice for Jo, and the three of them had a merry time together until Hannah appeared. Then, forgetting her foot, Meg rose quickly and cried out with pain.

When Laurie saw that she would not be able to walk, he immediately offered his grandfather's carriage.

"It's so early," said Jo, "you can't mean to go yet."

"I always go early," he said. "Please let me take you home."

So they set off home in the luxurious carriage, feeling very elegant. Laurie went on the box and the two girls chatted inside.

"I had a splendid time, did you?" said Jo.

"Yes, until I hurt myself," said Meg. "Sallie's friend, Annie Moffat, asked me to come and spend a week with her when Sallie does in the Spring. If only mother lets me go, it will be wonderful."

Then Jo told of her adventures, and by the time she had finished, they were home. They thanked Laurie and said goodnight, then crept into the house, hoping to disturb no one.

But two little voices immediately cried out.

"Tell us about the party! Tell us about the party!"

# Chapter 4

# *Being Neighbourly*

WHEN Mr March had lost his property in trying to help an unfortunate friend, the two eldest girls had begged to be allowed to help support themselves. Meg found a place as a nursery governess. She found being poor harder to bear than the others, because she could remember a time when their home was beautiful and they had wanted for nothing. And every day at the Kings' house she caught glimpses of dainty ball-dresses and bouquets, and overheard gossip about theatres, concerts, sleighing-parties and merry-making of all kinds.

Jo went to Aunt March, who needed someone to wait on her. She had offered to adopt one of the girls when the troubles came, and was very offended when her offer was turned down. She wouldn't speak to the family for a while, but eventually took Jo as a companion. Jo accepted the place when nothing better appeared, and surprised everyone by getting on remarkably well with her short-tempered relative.

The real attraction for Jo was the library, which had collected dust and spiders since Uncle March had died. The moment Aunt March took her nap or was busy with visitors, Jo hurried to this quiet place where she could wander and choose from the great wilderness of books.

Jo wanted to do something splendid and important, but her quick temper and sharp tongue were always getting her into scrapes. But the training she received at Aunt March's was just what she needed, and the thought that she was doing something to support herself pleased her.

Beth was too shy to go to school so had lessons at home, with her father. Even when he went away, and her mother's time was taken up with the Soldiers' Aid Societies, Beth went faithfully on by herself, doing the best she could, and helping Hannah keep the house neat and tidy for the others. Long, quiet days were spent with imaginary friends, or dressing and talking to her six dolls – not one whole or handsome one among them, for they had been passed on to her by her sisters. Beth often cried because she couldn't take music lessons or have a fine piano. She loved music dearly and practised patiently at their jingling old instrument.

If anybody had asked Amy what the greatest trial of her life was she would have answered, "My nose." When she was a baby, Jo had accidentally dropped her, and Amy insisted that the fall had ruined her nose for ever. It was not big or red, only rather flat, and nobody minded it but herself. She had a talent for drawing, and was never happier than when she was copying flowers or illustrating stories. Her teachers complained that, instead of doing her sums, she covered her slate with animals. But she was a favourite with her school-mates, being

good-tempered and able to please others without effort.

Everyone petted her, but one thing stopped her becoming too vain – she had to wear her cousin's clothes. They were well-made and little worn, but Amy suffered deeply at having to wear a red instead of a blue bonnet, or fussy aprons that did not fit. And this Winter her school dress was a dull purple with yellow dots, which looked awful to Amy's artistic eye.

One snowy afternoon Jo went out with a broom and a shovel and began to clear a path round the garden, for Beth to walk in when the sun came out. The garden separated the March's house from that of Mr Laurence, and both were in the suburb of the city. On one side of a low hedge was an old brown house, looking rather bare and shabby. On the other side was a stately stone mansion with a big coach-house, well-kept grounds, and lovely things inside which could be glimpsed between rich curtains. Yet it seemed a lonely, lifeless sort of house, for no children played on the lawn, no motherly face ever smiled at the windows, and few people went in and out except the old gentleman and his grandson.

To Jo, this fine house seemed a kind of enchanted palace, full of splendours and delights which no one enjoyed. She had long wanted to see inside and to know the 'Laurence boy', who looked as if he would like to be known, and since the party she had planned many ways of making friends with him. But he had not been seen lately, and Jo began to think he had gone away until one day she saw a face at an upper window, looking wistfully down at Beth and Amy snowballing one another.

"That boy needs some friends and some fun," Jo said to herself, "and I've a good mind to go over and tell the old gentleman so."

The plan of 'going over' had not been forgotten, and this snowy afternoon, Jo intended to see what could be done. She saw Mr Laurence drive off, then dug her way down to the hedge and paused to look.

All was quiet at the house. Curtains were down at the lower windows, the servants were out of sight. But a curly black head was leaning on a thin hand at the upper window.

Jo threw up a handful of soft snow.

Immediately the face showed a smile.

Jo waved her broom and called out, "How do you? Are you sick?"

Laurie opened the window and croaked, "Better, thank you. I've had a bad cold and been shut up a week."

"I'm sorry. What do you amuse yourself with?"

"Nothing. It's very dull," he said.

"Don't you read?"

"Not much. They won't let me."

"Can't somebody read to you?"

"Grandpa does, sometimes, but my books don't interest him."

"Have someone come and see you then," said Jo.

"I don't know anyone."

"You know us," began Jo, then laughed and stopped.

"So I do!" cried Laurie. "Will you come, please?"

"I'll come if Mother will let me," said Jo. "I'll go and ask her. Shut the window like a good boy and wait until I come."

Jo shouldered her broom and marched into the house.

Laurie was excited at the idea of having company and began to get ready. He brushed his hair, put on a fresh collar and tried to tidy up his room. Soon after, the doorbell rang and a voice asked for "Mr Laurie." Then a surprised servant ran up to announce a young lady.

"Show her up, it's Miss Jo," said Laurie.

Moments later, Jo appeared with a covered dish in one hand and Beth's three kittens in the other. "Mother sends her love," she said. "Meg wanted me to bring some of her blancmange, and Beth thought

her cats would be comforting. I knew you'd laugh, but I couldn't refuse."

Laurie *did* laugh, but he also forgot to be shy, so Beth's funny loan was just the thing.

"That looks too pretty to eat," he said, smiling as Jo uncovered the blancmange, which was surrounded by green leaves and scarlet flowers.

"Tell the girl to put it away for your tea," said Jo. "It will slip down easily without hurting your sore throat. What a cosy room this is!"

"It would be, if it was kept nice, but the maids are lazy."

"I'll make it right in two minutes," said Jo. "It only needs the hearth brushed, so – and the things put straight on the mantelpiece, so – and the books put here and your sofa turned from the light, and the pillows plumped up a bit. There, now you're fixed."

And so he was, for Jo had whisked things into place as she talked.

"How kind you are," he said.

"Shall I read to you?" asked Jo.

"If you don't mind, I'd rather talk," answered Laurie.

"I'll talk all day if you set me going," said Jo. "Beth says I never know when to stop."

"Is Beth the rosy one who stays at home?"

"Yes, that's Beth. She's my girl, and a good one she is, too."

"The pretty one is Meg and the curly-haired one is Amy, I believe?"

"How did you find that out?"

Laurie's face coloured up. "I hear you calling to one another. I can't help looking over at your house, you always seem to be having such good times. Sometimes you forget to put down your curtain at the window where the flowers are, and when the lamps are lit it's like looking at a picture to see the fire, and you all round it with your mother. I can't help watching. I haven't got a mother, you know."

There was a hungry look in his eyes that went straight to Jo's heart.

"We'll never draw that curtain any more," she said. "I wish, instead of peeping, you'd come over and see us. We could have such a jolly time. Wouldn't your grandpa let you?"

"I think he would if your mother asked him. He's just afraid I might be a bother to strangers."

"We're not strangers, we're neighbours, and you wouldn't be a bother."

"Grandpa lives among his books," said Laurie, "and Mr Brooke, my tutor, doesn't stay here. I've no one to go about with, so I stop at home and get on as well as I can."

"That's bad. You ought to make an effort and go visiting everywhere you're asked, then you'll have plenty of friends."

"Do you like your school?" asked Laurie.

"I don't go to school, I wait on my aunt," said Jo.

She described the fidgety old lady and her fat poodle, the parrot that talked Spanish, and the library where she loved to go. And when she told Laurie about the prim old gentleman who once came to woo Aunt March and how, in the middle of a fine speech, Polly had tweaked off his wig, the boy lay back and laughed until the tears ran down his cheeks.

"Tell me more, please," he said, his face red with merriment.

So Jo told him about their plays and plans, and their hopes and fears for Father. Then they got to talking about books and Jo discovered that Laurie loved them as well as she did, and had read even more than herself.

"Come down and see ours," he said. "Grandpa is out, so you needn't be afraid."

"I'm not afraid of anything," replied Jo, tossing her head.

"I don't believe you are!" said Laurie, looking at her with admiration.

He led the way from room to room, letting Jo examine what took her fancy, until they came to the library. There, Jo clapped her hands and pranced, as she always did when she was delighted. It was lined with books, and there were pictures and statues and little cabinets full of coins and curiosities.

Jo sank into a velvet chair. "Theodore Laurence," she said, "you ought to be the happiest boy in the world."

"A fellow can't live on books," said Laurie.

Before he could say any more, a bell rang.

Jo flew out of the chair. "Mercy me! It's your grandpa!"

"What if it is? You're not afraid of anything," said Laurie, looking wicked.

"I think I am a little afraid of him, but I don't know why I should be. Marmee said I might come, and I don't think you're any worse for it."

"I'm a great deal better for it," said Laurie.

"The doctor to see you sir." The maid beckoned as she spoke.

"Would you mind if I left you for a moment?" said Laurie.

"Don't mind me. I'm as happy as a cricket here," said Jo.

Laurie went away and Jo was staring at a fine portrait of the old gentleman when the door opened again. Without turning, she said, "I'm sure I shouldn't be afraid of him because he's got kind eyes, though his mouth is grim, and he looks as if he has a will of his own. He isn't as handsome as *my* grandfather, but I like him."

"Thank you, ma'am," said a gruff voice behind her, and there, to her great dismay, stood Mr Laurence.

Jo blushed until she couldn't blush any redder. She wanted to run away, but that would be cowardly so she decided to stay. She saw that the eyes under the bushy eyebrows were even kinder than the painted ones, and that there was a sly twinkle in them.

"So you're not afraid of me, eh?" said the gruff voice.

"Not much, sir," said Jo.

"And you don't think me as handsome as your grandfather?"

"Not quite, sir."

"But you like me, in spite of it?"

"Yes, I do, sir."

The answer pleased the old gentleman.

He gave a short laugh and shook hands with her. "You've got your grandfather's spirit," he said.

"Thank you, sir."

"What have you been doing to my grandson?"

"Trying to be neighbourly, sir." Jo told how the visit came about.

"You think he needs cheering up a bit, do you?"

"Yes, sir, he seems a littie lonely," said Jo. "We're only girls, but we'd be glad to help, for we haven't forgotten the splendid Christmas present you sent us."

"That was the boy. How is the poor woman?"

"Doing nicely, sir."

"Tell your mother I shall come and see her some fine day. Now, there's the tea bell. Come down, and go on being neighbourly." He offered her his arm.

Laurie came running downstairs and was astonished by the sight of Jo, arm-in-arm with his grandfather. "I didn't know you'd come home, sir," he said.

The old gentleman did not say much over tea, but he watched the two young people chatting happily. He saw the colour and life in the boy's face and heard the merriment in his laugh.

'She's right,' he thought. 'The lad *is*

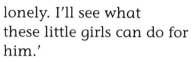

lonely. I'll see what these little girls can do for him.'

After tea, Laurie took Jo to the conservatory and cut some flowers. "Please give these to your mother," he said, "and tell her I like the medicine she sends me very much."

They found Mr Laurence in the drawing room where Jo quickly became interested in a grand piano which stood open.

"Do you play?" she asked Laurie.

"Sometimes," he answered, modestly.

"Please do now, I want to hear it so I can tell Beth."

So Laurie played and Jo listened. She wished Beth could hear him but did not say so, only praised him until his grandfather said, "That will do, young lady. His music isn't bad, but I hope he will do as well in more important things. Going now? Well, I hope you'll come again. Goodnight, Doctor Jo."

He shook hands kindly but looked as if something didn't please him. When they were in the hall, Jo asked Laurie if she had said anything wrong.

"No," said Laurie. "It was me. He doesn't like to hear me play."

"Why not?"

"I'll tell you some day. You will come again, I hope?"

"If you promise to come and see us after you're well."

"I will."

"Goodnight, Laurie."

"Goodnight, Jo, goodnight!"

When Jo told of her adventures, each member of the family wanted to go and visit the big house. Mrs March wanted to talk of her father with the old man who had not forgotten him; Meg longed to walk in the conservatory; Beth sighed for the grand piano; and Amy was eager to see the fine pictures and statues.

"Mother, why didn't Mr Laurence like to have Laurie play?" asked Jo.

"I think it was because his son, Laurie's father, married an Italian lady, a musician, which did not please the old man. He didn't like her, and never saw his son after they were married. They both died when Laurie was little, so his grandfather took him home. The boy was born in Italy, but is not very strong, and the old man is afraid of losing him. Laurie's love of music comes from his mother, but I expect his grandfather is afraid he may want to be a musician."

"How silly!" said Jo. "Let him be a musician if he wants to be. Don't send him to college when he hates to go. Marmee, he may come over and see us, mayn't he?"

"Yes, Jo," said her mother. "Your little friend is very welcome."

# Chapter 5

# Beth's Wish Come True

THE girls found old Mr Laurence a little frightening, but after he had called, said some funny things to each of them, and talked over old times with their mother, nobody felt afraid of him except Beth.

Laurie found these busy, lively girls delightful. He was tired of books and found people so interesting now that his tutor, Mr Brooke, was forced to make unsatisfactory reports about his pupil, who was always playing truant and running over to the Marches' house.

"Never mind, let him take a holiday and make it up afterwards," said the old gentleman.

What good times they had! Plays and sleigh-rides and skating, pleasant evenings in the old parlour, and now and then little parties at the great house. Meg could walk in the conservatory whenever she liked, Jo browsed in the library to her heart's content, Amy copied pictures, and Laurie played lord of the manor in the most delightful style.

Only Beth could not pluck up courage to go to the big house. She went once with Jo, but the old gentleman, not realising how timid she was, said "Hey!" so loudly that she ran away. After that, nobody could persuade her to go until Mr Laurence, hearing about this, set about mending matters. On one visit to Mrs March, he led the conversation to music and talked about great singers he had seen and fine organs

he had heard. Beth found it impossible to stay in her corner and crept nearer and nearer to hear. She listened at the back of his chair, her eyes wide open and her cheeks red with excitement.

He talked on about Laurie's lessons and teachers, and then, as if the idea had just occurred to him, said to Mrs March, "The boy does not play as much now and the piano suffers from lack of use. Would some of your girls like to run over and practise on it now and then, just to keep it in tune?"

Beth took a step forward. The thought of practising on that splendid instrument quite took her breath away.

Mr Laurence went on, "They needn't see or speak to anyone. I'm always out or in my study, Laurie is out a great deal, and the servants are never near the drawing room after nine o'clock. Please tell the young ladies what I say, and if they don't care to come, then never mind."

At this moment, a little hand slipped into his. It was Beth's.

"Oh, sir, they do care," she said. "Very much!"

"Are you the musical girl?" he asked softly.

"I'm Beth. I love it dearly, and I shall come."

So next day, after seeing both the old and the young gentleman go out, Beth went across to the big house. She went in at the side door and found her way to the drawing

room. There stood the grand piano. At last Beth was able to touch the instrument – and straight away forgot all her fears and everything except the delight which the music gave her.

After that, she slipped through the hedge and into the big house nearly every day. It was as if that great drawing room was haunted by a tuneful spirit who came and went unseen. Beth never knew that Mr Laurence often opened his study door to listen to her playing or that Laurie stood guard in the hall to keep servants away. She never suspected that the new songs she found in the rack were put there especially for her.

"Mother, I'm going to work Mr Laurence a pair of slippers," she said one evening. "He's so kind to me, I must thank him. Can I do it?"

"Yes, dear," said Mrs March. "It will please him very much. The girls will help you and I will pay for the making up." She took extra pleasure granting Beth's requests because the little girl seldom asked anything for herself.

So the pattern was chosen, the materials bought and the slippers begun. Pansies on a deeper purple background seemed just the thing, and Beth worked away early and late. She was a nimble little needle-woman and they were soon finished. Then she wrote a short note and, with Laurie's help, smuggled them into the old man's study one morning before he was up.

On the afternoon of the following day, Beth went out on an errand and was coming back up the street when she saw four heads popping in and out of the parlour windows. The moment they saw her, hands were waved and voices shouted, "There's a letter from the old gentleman, come quick and read it!"

Beth hurried to the house where she was led into the parlour, everyone saying at once, "Look there! Look there!" Beth looked and turned pale with delight and surprise. For there stood a little cabinet piano with a letter lying on the glossy lid, addressed to 'Miss Elizabeth March'.

"For me?" gasped Beth, holding on to Jo.

"Yes, all for you, my precious!" said Jo. "Isn't he the dearest old man in the world? Open your letter, we're dying to know what he says."

"You read it, Jo," said Beth, her voice shaking. "I can't."

So Jo opened the paper and, starting to laugh, read, "'Miss March. Dear Madam – '"

"How nice it sounds," said Amy. "I wish someone would write to me like that."

Then Jo went on:

"'I have had many pairs of slippers in my life but never any that suited me so well as yours. They will always remind me of the gentle giver. I like to pay my debts, so I know you will allow the 'old gentleman' to send you something that once belonged to the little granddaughter he lost. With hearty thanks and best wishes, I remain your grateful friend, James Laurence.'

"There, Beth, that's an honour to be proud of." Jo put an arm around her sister who was trembling with excitement. "Laurie told me how fond Mr Laurence used to be of the little child that died, and how he kept all her things carefully. Just think, he's given you her piano. That comes of having big blue eyes and loving music."

"Try it, honey," said Hannah, who always shared in the family's joys and sorrows.

So Beth tried it, lovingly touching the beautiful black and white keys and pressing the bright pedals, and everyone thought it was the most perfect piano they had ever heard.

"You will have to go and thank him," said

Jo, meaning it as a joke, for she knew how shy Beth was.

But Beth amazed the whole family by saying, "Yes, I mean to. I'll go now before I get frightened by thinking about it."

And she walked down the garden, through the hedge and in at the Laurence's door. The girls were made speechless by this miracle.

They would have been still more amazed if they had seen what Beth did afterwards. She knocked at the study door and, after a gruff voice said, "Come in," went right up to Mr Laurence and held her hand out.

"I came to say thank you, sir, for – " she began. But she didn't finish. He looked so friendly that she forgot her speech, and only remembering that he had lost the little girl he loved, she put both arms round his neck and kissed him.

If the roof of the house had suddenly flown off, the old gentleman wouldn't have been more astonished. But he liked it – oh, dear, yes! All his crustiness vanished and Beth ceased to be afraid of him from that moment on.

When she went home, he walked with her to her gate where he shook hands and touched his hat before marching back again, looking very tall and handsome. When the girls saw this, Jo danced a jig, Amy nearly fell out of the window with surprise and Meg said, "Well, I do believe the world is coming to an end!"

# Chapter 6

# Shame for Amy

"I NEED some money," Amy said one day.

"Why?" asked Meg.

"For some pickled limes," said Amy. "The girls at school are always buying them and, unless you want to be thought mean, you must do it, too."

"How much do you need?" asked Meg, taking out her purse.

"A quarter would more than do it."

"Here's the money. Make it last as long as you can."

Next day, Amy was rather late at school but could not resist displaying a moist brown-paper parcel before putting it into her desk. During the next few minutes, the rumour that Amy March had twenty-four delicious limes went round her friends. Katy Brown immediately invited Amy to her next party. Mary Kingsley insisted on lending Amy her watch for the morning. And Jenny Snow offered to give Amy the answers to some very difficult sums. But Amy had not forgotten Miss Snow's recent remarks about 'some people whose noses were too flat to smell other people's limes', and instantly crushed the girl's hopes by saying "You needn't be so polite all of a sudden, for you won't get any."

Later that morning, an important person visited the school, and Amy's beautifully drawn maps received praise. This honour rankled Miss Snow and caused Miss March to behave like a young peacock. But pride goes before a fall and Miss Snow got her revenge. No sooner had the guest gone than Jenny, pretending to ask an important question, managed to inform Mr Davis, the teacher that Amy March had pickled limes in her desk.

Now Mr Davis had declared limes a forbidden article and had promised to punish the first person who was found breaking the law. Unfortunately, he was also in a bad temper that morning.

"Young ladies, attention, please!" he called.

The buzz round the classroom ceased and everyone looked up.

"Miss March, come to the desk."

Amy rose calmly, but with the limes weighing on her conscience.

"And bring the limes you have in your desk!" snapped Mr Davis.

"Don't take them all!" whispered her neighbour.

Amy hastily shook out six, then took the rest to Mr Davis.

"Is that all?" he said.

"Er – not quite," said Amy.

"Bring the rest immediately."

With a despairing glance at her friends, she obeyed.

"Now," said Mr Davis, "throw them out of the window, two by two."

Her face red and angry, Amy went to and from the window until all the limes were gone. Shouts of delight came from outside

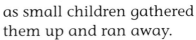

as small children gathered them up and ran away.

"Young ladies," said Mr Davis, "I will not have my rules broken. Miss March, hold out your hand."

Amy jumped and put both hands behind her.

"Your hand, Miss March!"

Too proud to cry or plead, Amy stood without flinching as the tingling blows came down on her palm. They were neither many nor heavy, but for the first time in her life she had been struck, and the disgrace she felt was as deep as if he had knocked her down.

"You will stand on the platform for the rest of the morning," said Mr Davis.

That was dreadful. To face the whole school with that shame fresh upon her seemed more than Amy could bear. She wanted to cry, and only a bitter sense of wrong and the thought of Jenny Snow stopped her. Fifteen long minutes of shame and pain followed before the morning ended.

"You can go, Miss March," said Mr Davis, looking uncomfortable.

He did not soon forget the reproachful look Amy gave him as she snatched up her things and, without a word to anyone, left that place 'for ever' as she passionately declared to herself.

She was in a sad state when she got home. Mrs March did not say much but looked disturbed as she comforted her little daughter.

"You can have a vacation from school," Mrs March told Amy that evening, "but I want you to study each day with Beth. I don't approve of corporal punishment and I don't like Mr Davis' manner of teaching, so I'll ask your father's advice before I send you anywhere else."

"That's good," said Amy. "I wish all the girls would leave and spoil his old school! It's maddening to think of all those lovely limes."

"I'm not sorry you lost them," said Mrs March, "for you broke the rules and deserved some punishment."

"Do you mean you're glad I was disgraced before the whole school?" cried Amy, who had expected nothing but sympathy.

"I should not have chosen that way of mending a fault," replied her mother, "but I'm not sure it won't do you more good than a milder method. You're getting to be rather conceited, my dear, and it's time it was corrected. You have a good many little gifts and virtues, but there is no need to parade them."

# Chapter 7

# An Angry Jo

"GIRLS, where are you going?" asked Amy one Saturday afternoon. "Little girls shouldn't ask questions," Jo answered sharply.

Amy turned to Meg. "Do tell me! You could let me go too!"

"I can't, dear, because you're not invited," began Meg.

"Now Meg, be quiet," broke in Jo, "or you will spoil it all."

"You're going somewhere with Laurie, I know you are!" said Amy.

"Yes, we are. Now be still and stop bothering," said Jo.

"I know! You're going to see the *Seven Castles* at the theatre, and I *shall* go because Mother said I could see it."

"You can go next week with Beth and Hannah," said Meg, soothingly.

"I want to go with you and Laurie! Please let me, Meg!"

"Suppose we take her," began Meg.

"If *she* goes, I shan't, and Laurie won't like it," warned Jo. "He only invited us, it will be rude to drag Amy along."

This angered Amy who began to put her boots on. "I *shall* go. Meg says I may and – "

"You just stay where you are!" scolded Jo.

They left their sister wailing.

"You'll be sorry for this, Jo March!" Amy shouted.

"Fiddlesticks!" returned Jo, slamming the door. They had a charming time at the theatre, but Jo's pleasure was spoilt a little by wondering what her sister would to to 'make her sorry'.

She found out the next day.

Beth, Amy and Meg were sitting together when Jo burst into the room.

"Has anyone taken my book?" she asked, breathlessly.

Meg and Beth said, "No," at once. Amy poked the fire and said nothing.

"Amy, you've got it!"

"No, I haven't."

"That's a fib!" cried Jo, taking her by the shoulders. "You know something about it and you'd better tell me, or I'll make you!"

"Do what you like," said Amy. "You'll never see your silly book again."

"Why not?"

"I burned it."

"What! My little book I was so fond of and working to finish before Father got home?" Jo's face turned pale. "Have you really burned it?"

"Yes! I told you I'd make you pay for being so cross yesterday – "

Amy got no further for she found herself being shaken until her teeth rattled. "You wicked, wicked girl!" cried Jo, weeping with grief and anger. "I can never write it again and I'll never forgive you as long as I live." And she rushed out of the room.

Mrs March soon made Amy see the great wrong she had done her sister. Jo's book was the pride of her heart. It was only a few little fairy tales, but Jo had written them herself

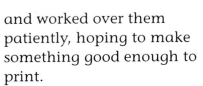

and worked over them patiently, hoping to make something good enough to print.

When the tea bell rang, Jo appeared, looking so grim that it took all Amy's courage to say, "Please forgive me, Jo. I'm very, very sorry."

"I shall never forgive you," was Jo's stern answer.

Words were wasted when Jo was in that mood, so no one spoke of the great trouble again. It was not a happy evening, and as Jo said goodnight, Mrs March whispered gently, "My dear, don't let the sun go down on your anger."

But Jo shook her head and muttered, "She doesn't deserve to be forgiven." And she marched off to bed.

Next day, Jo looked like a thundercloud. "Everybody is so hateful, I'll ask Laurie to go skating," she said to herself.

Amy heard the clash of skates. "She promised to take me next time!" she complained. "But it's no use asking such a cross-patch."

"It's hard to forgive what you did," said Meg. "Go after them, wait until Laurie has cheered her up, then do some kind thing."

"I'll try," said Amy.

It was not far to the river. Jo saw Amy coming and turned her back. Laurie was busy checking the ice by skating carefully along the shore.

"I'll go on to the first bend and see if it's all right before we race," Amy heard him say to Jo. And he shot away.

Amy stamped her feet and blew on her fingers as she put her skates on. Jo heard but did not turn round, just slowly zig-zagged down the river.

"Keep near the shore, it isn't safe in the middle," Laurie called.

Jo heard him, but Amy did not. Jo glanced over her shoulder, and the little demon inside her said, "Let her take care of herself."

Laurie had vanished round the bend, Jo was just at the turn, and Amy was striking out towards the smoother ice in the middle of the river.

Something made Jo turn round – just in time to see Amy throw up her hands and go crashing through the rotten ice. Amy gave a cry that made Jo's heart stand still with fear. She tried to call Laurie but her voice was gone, and for a second she could only stand and stare terror-stricken at the little blue hood above the black water.

Something rushed by her and Laurie shouted, "Bring a rail, quick!"

Lying flat on the ice, Laurie held Amy up until Jo dragged a rail from the fence and they got the child out, more frightened than hurt.

Shivering and crying, Amy was taken home, where she fell asleep, rolled in blankets, before a hot fire. Jo's dress was torn, her hands cut and bruised from wrenching the rail from the fence. She had hardly spoken a word, but when the house was quiet, Mrs March called Jo to her and began to bandage her hands.

"Are you sure she's safe?" whispered Jo.

"Quite safe, dear. You were sensible to get her home quickly."

"Laurie did it all," said Jo. "Mother, if she should die, it would be my fault." Tears rolled down her cheeks. "It's my dreadful temper!"

"You think your temper is the worst in the world," said her mother, "but mine used to be just like it."

"Yours, Mother? Why, you're never angry!"

"I'm angry nearly every day of my life, Jo, but I've learned not to show it. I've learned to check the hasty words that rise to my lips."

"Oh, Mother, if I could be half as good as you, I should be satisfied," said Jo.

"I hope you'll be a great deal better, dear, but you must keep watch over your temper."

Amy stirred in her sleep and Jo looked at her. "I let the sun go down on my anger," she said. "I wouldn't forgive her, and today, if it hadn't been for Laurie, it might have been too late! How could I have been so wicked?" She stroked the wet hair scattered on the pillow.

As if she heard, Amy opened her eyes and held out her arms with a smile that went straight to Jo's heart. Neither spoke, but hugged one another close, and everything was forgiven in one kiss.

# Chapter 8

# Meg goes to Vanity Fair

ANNIE MOFFAT did not forget her promise and one April day, Meg went to stay with her for 'a whole fortnight of fun', as Jo had described it.

Meg was rather daunted at first by the big house and its elegant occupants, but she soon began to imitate the manners and conversation of those about her. She put on little airs and graces, crimped her hair and talked about the fashions as well as she could. The more she saw of Annie's pretty things, the more Meg sighed to be rich.

They shopped, walked, rode, went to theatres and operas, or had fun at home in the evenings, for Annie had many friends and knew how to entertain them. Her older sisters were fine young ladies, and one was engaged, which was extremely romantic, Meg thought. Mr Moffat was a fat, jolly gentleman, Mrs Moffat a fat, jolly lady. Everyone petted Meg, and 'Daisy', as they called her, was all set to have her head turned.

When the evening for the 'small party' came, Meg wore her white tarlatan dress, which looked older, limper and shabbier than ever against Sallie's crisp new one. No one said a word about it, but Sallie offered to do her hair and Annie to tie her sash, while Belle, the engaged sister, praised her white arms. Meg was sure they pitied her for her poverty, and her heart felt heavy. Then the maid brought in a box of flowers.

"They are for Miss March," she said, "and here's a note."

"What fun!" cried the girls. "Who are they from?"

"The note is from Mother and the flowers from Laurie," said Meg, feeling almost happy again.

"Oh, indeed," said Annie, with a funny look, as Meg slipped the note into her pocket.

Meg enjoyed herself very much that evening. But later, when she was sitting in the conservatory waiting for someone to bring her an ice, she heard a voice say, "How old is she?"

"Sixteen or seventeen, I think," replied another voice.

"It would be a grand thing for one of those girls, wouldn't it? Sallie says they are very friendly, and the old man quite dotes on them."

"Mrs M. has made her plans, I dare say. The girl evidently doesn't think of it yet," said Mrs Moffat.

"She told that fib about her mamma as if she did know, and coloured up quite prettily. Poor thing! Do you think she'd be offended if we offered to lend her a dress for Thursday?" asked another voice.

"She's proud, but I don't believe she'd mind, for that dowdy tarlatan is all she's got."

"I shall ask young Laurence, as a compliment to her, and we'll have some fun about it afterwards."

Meg was angry and disgusted by the gossip and it spoilt her evening. She was very glad when it was all over and she was in her bed where her hot cheeks were cooled by a few tears.

She had a restless night and got up heavy-eyed. Something in the manner of her friends struck Meg at once. They treated her with more respect, she thought, and were plainly curious. She began to understand when Miss Belle said, with a sentimental air, "Daisy, dear, we've sent an invitation to your friend, Mr Laurence, for Thursday."

Meg decided to tease them. "You're very kind, but I'm afraid he won't come. He's too old."

"What do you mean? How old is he?" asked Miss Clara.

"Nearly seventy, I believe."

"You sly creature!" laughed Miss Belle. "We meant the young man."

"There isn't any. Laurie is only a little boy."

"About your age?" Nan said.

"Nearer Jo's. I'm seventeen in August."

"It's nice of him to send you flowers," said Annie.

"He often does, to all of us. My mother and old Mr Laurence are friends, so it's quite natural that we children should play together."

"What will you wear on Thursday?" asked Sallie.

"My old white one again," said Meg, "if I can mend it. It got torn."

"Why don't you send home for another?" said Sallie.

"I haven't got any other." It cost Meg a lot to say that.

"Only that?" said Sallie. "How funny – "

Belle broke in with, "I've got a sweet blue silk dress which I've outgrown, Meg, and you shall wear it to please me."

"You're very kind, but – "

"Please do," Belle said. "You'll be a regular little beauty with a touch here and a touch there."

Meg couldn't refuse the kind offer, and the desire to see if she could really be a 'little beauty' caused her to forget all her uncomfortable feelings towards the Moffats.

On the Thursday evening, Belle and her maid turned Meg into a fine lady. They crimped and curled her hair, powdered her neck and arms, touched her lips with coralline salve to make them redder, then laced her into the sky-blue dress. It was so tight Meg could hardly breathe, and so low in the neck that she blushed at herself in the mirror. Bracelets, a necklace, a brooch and earrings were added, and a lace handkerchief, a fan, and a bouquet in a silver holder finished her off.

Several young gentlemen, who had only stared before, asked to be introduced. Young ladies who had taken no notice before were very affectionate all of a sudden. Interested old ladies enquired who she was.

It was a wonderful feeling for Meg, acting the part of a 'fine lady'. She flirted with her fan, and laughed at the feeble jokes of a young gentleman who tried to be witty. But then she saw Laurie. He was staring at her with surprise and disapproval. He bowed and smiled, but something in his eyes made her blush and wish she had her old dress on. She saw Belle nudge Annie, and both glance from her to Laurie.

"I'm glad you came," Meg said to Laurie in her most grown-up voice. "I was afraid you wouldn't."

"Jo wanted me to come, to tell her how you looked."

"What will you tell her?"

"I shall say I didn't know you, for you look so grown up and unlike yourself. I'm

quite afraid of you," he said, fumbling with his gloves.

"How silly! The girls dressed me up for fun, and I rather like it. Wouldn't Jo stare if she saw me?"

"Yes, I think she would," said Laurie, gravely.

"Don't you like me so?" asked Meg.

"No, I don't," came the blunt reply.

"Why not?" Meg asked anxiously.

"I don't like fuss and feathers."

It was too much for Meg. "You're the rudest boy ever!" she said.

She went and stood by a window, half hidden by the curtains. As she stood there, Major Lincoln passed by, and she heard him say to his mother, "They're making a fool of that little girl. She's nothing but a doll."

"Oh, dear!" sighed Meg. "I wish I'd worn my own things."

Turning, she saw Laurie. "Please forgive my rudeness and come and dance with me," he said.

Meg tried to look offended.

"Please come," he said. "I don't like your gown, but I do think you are – just splendid!"

Meg smiled, then whispered, "Take care my skirt doesn't trip you up. It's the plague of my life and I was a goose to wear it."

They twirled round merrily, more friendly than ever.

"Laurie, please do me a favour," said Meg. "Please don't tell them at home about my dress tonight. They won't understand the joke and it will worry Mother. I'll tell them myself and confess how silly I've been."

"I give you my word I'll say nothing," said Laurie.

He did not speak to her again until supper-time when he saw her drinking champagne with Ned and his friend Fisher, who were behaving 'like a pair of fools' as

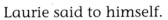

Laurie said to himself.

"You'll have a splitting headache tomorrow if you drink much of that," he whispered to Meg. "Your mother doesn't like it, you know."

"I'm not Meg tonight," she said. "I'm a doll who does crazy things. Tomorrow I'll put away my fuss and feathers and be good again."

Meg was sick all the next day, and on Saturday went home, quite tired of her fortnight's fun. She spoke over and over again of the charming time she'd had, but something seemed to weigh upon her spirits. After the younger girls had gone to bed, Meg sat next to her mother and told her and Jo how she'd been powdered and frizzled and made to look like a doll. And how she'd drunk champagne and tried to flirt and was altogether dreadful.

"There is something more," said Mrs March, smoothing Meg's soft cheek which suddenly grew rosy.

"Yes, it's very silly but I want to tell it," said Meg, "because I hate to have people say and think such things about us and Laurie."

Then she told the various bits of gossip she had heard at the Moffats.

"Well, if that isn't the greatest rubbish I've ever heard!" cried Jo. "Just wait until *I* see Annie Moffat! The idea of having 'plans' and being kind because he's rich and may marry us! Won't he laugh when I tell him!"

"If you tell Laurie, I'll never forgive you!" said Meg, looking distressed. "She mustn't, must she, Mother?"

"No, never repeat foolish gossip, and forget it as soon as you can," said Mrs March. "I was unwise to let you go, Meg."

"I'll forget the bad and remember the good," said Meg. "Mother, do you have 'plans', as Mrs Moffat said?"

"All mothers do, my dear. I want my daughters to be admired, loved and respected, and one day to be well and wisely married. I am ambitious for you, my dears, but not to have you marry rich men merely because they are rich. I would rather see you poor men's wives if you were happy and contented than queens on thrones without self-respect and peace."

"Poor girls don't stand a chance, Belle says," sighed Meg.

"Then we'll be old maids," said Jo.

"Right, Jo. Better to be happy old maids than unhappy wives," said Mrs March, decidedly. "Your father and I trust that our daughters, whether married or single, will be the pride and comfort of our lives."

"We will, Marmee, we will!" cried both, with all their hearts.

# Chapter 9

# Experiments

"THE first of June, the Kings are off to the sea-shore tomorrow, and I'm free!" cried Meg. "Three months vacation! How I shall enjoy it!"

"Aunt March went today," said Jo. "Oh, be joyful!"

"What will you do all your vacation?" asked Amy.

"I shall lie a-bed late and do nothing," said Meg.

"I've got a heap of books to read," said Jo.

"Let's not do any lessons, Beth," proposed Amy. "We'll play all the time, and rest, as the girls mean to."

"I will if Mother doesn't mind," said Beth.

"May we, Mother?" asked Meg, turning to Mrs March.

"You may try your experiment for a week," said Mrs March. "I think by Saturday night you'll find that all play and no work is as bad as all work and no play."

"Oh, no! It will be delicious, I'm sure," said Meg.

Next day, Meg appeared at ten o'clock and ate breakfast alone. It did not taste as good and the room seemed lonely and untidy, for Jo had not filled the vases, Beth had not dusted, and Amy's books lay scattered about.

Jo spent the morning on the river with Laurie, and the afternoon reading a book sitting in the apple tree. Beth began by rummaging everything out of her big cupboard, but got tired and left it half done

and topsy-turvy. She went to her music, rejoicing that she had no dishes to wash. Amy sat under the honeysuckles to draw, hoping someone would see and ask who the young artist was. As no one appeared but a daddy-long-legs, she went for a walk, got caught in a shower and came home dripping.

At tea-time, all agreed that it had been a delightful but unusually long day. Meg, who went shopping in the afternoon, discovered that the dress she had bought wouldn't wash, which made her slightly cross. Jo had burnt the skin off her nose boating and got a raging headache by reading too long. Beth was worried by the confusion in her cupboard, and Amy regretted the damage done to her frock by the rain for now she had nothing to wear to Katy Brown's party the next day.

But these were mere trifles, they told their mother, and the experiment was working well. Mrs March smiled and said nothing.

The days kept getting longer. Meg put out some of her sewing, and then found time hang so heavily that she began snipping and spoiling her clothes in her attempt to improve their appearance. Jo was sick of books, and got so fidgety that even Laurie quarrelled with her. Beth kept forgetting that it was to be all play and no work, and now and then fell back into her old ways. Even so, the irritable atmosphere affected her. Amy fared worst of all. She didn't like

dolls, thought fairy tales childish and got bored with drawing.

No one would admit they were tired of the experiment but, by Friday night, each was glad the week was nearly over. Hoping to make them learn the lesson more deeply, Mrs March gave Hannah a holiday.

When they got up on Saturday there was no fire in the kitchen, no breakfast in the dining room, and no Mother anywhere to be seen.

"Mercy, what has happened?" cried Jo.

Meg ran upstairs, and soon came back again looking relieved but bewildered, and a little ashamed. "Mother isn't sick, only tired. She's staying in her room today. We must take care of ourselves."

"Good, I'm aching for something to do," said Jo.

Beth and Amy set the table while Meg and Jo got breakfast.

"I'll take some up to Mother," said Meg.

The tea was very bitter and the omelette scorched, but Mrs March did not complain, only chuckled to herself after Meg was gone.

Meg put the parlour in order by whisking the litter under the sofa and shutting the blinds to save the trouble of dusting. Jo, with perfect faith in her own powers as cook, invited Laurie to dinner.

"There's corn beef and plenty of potatoes, and I shall get some asparagus and a lobster," she told Meg. "We'll have blancmange and strawberries for dessert, and coffee too."

"Get what you like and don't disturb me, I'm going out for dinner," said Mrs March when Jo spoke to her.

Jo went back downstairs to find Beth

sobbing over Pip, the canary, who lay dead in the cage.

"It's all my fault, I forgot him!" wailed Beth. "There isn't a seed or drop of water – oh, Pip! How could I be so cruel!"

Leaving the others to console Beth, Jo went to the kitchen which was in a state of confusion. She put on a big apron and piled the dishes up ready for washing – and then discovered that the fire was out. Jo slammed the stove door open and poked amongst the cinders, then decided to go to the shops while the water heated. She bought a very young lobster, some very old asparagus, and two boxes of acid strawberries. She trudged home and, by the time she had got cleared up, the dinner arrived and the stove was red hot. Hannah had left a pan of bread to rise, and Meg had set it on the hearth to rise and then forgot it so that it ran all over the pan.

Mrs March went out, after peeping here and there to see how matters went, and a sense of helplessness fell upon the girls. A few minutes later, Miss Crocker appeared and said she'd come to dinner. This lady was a spinster with a sharp nose and inquisitive eyes, who saw everything and gossiped about all she saw. They disliked her but had been taught to be kind, so Meg tried to entertain her while she asked questions and criticized everything.

Jo did her best, but the dinner became a standing joke. The lobster was a great mystery to her but she hammered and poked until it was unshelled, then concealed its meagre portions in amongst the lettuce leaves. The asparagus burned and the potatoes weren't properly cooked. The blancmange was lumpy and the strawberries were not as ripe as they looked. Poor Jo was mortified at having spent all morning for nothing.

Amy giggled, Meg looked distressed, Miss Crocker made a face, and Laurie talked and laughed to cheer everybody up. Jo's last hope was the fruit. She had sugared it well and there was a jug of cream to go with it. Miss Crocker tasted first, then drank some water hastily. Jo, who had refused, thinking there might not be enough, glanced at Laurie who was eating away manfully but with his eyes fixed on the dish. Amy took a heaped spoonful, choked, hid her face in the napkin, and ran from the table.

"What is it?" said Jo.

"Salt instead of sugar," replied Meg, "and the cream is sour."

Jo groaned, fell back in her chair, caught the look in Laurie's eye – and began to laugh. She laughed until the tears ran down her cheeks. So did everyone else, even Miss Crocker!

It took them all afternoon to clear up the mess.

"What a dreadful day!" began Jo.

"It has seemed shorter than usual, but *so* uncomfortable," said Meg.

"Not a bit like home," added Amy.

Mrs March came home and took her place among them.

"Are you satisfied with your experiment, girls, or do you want another week of it?" she asked.

"I don't!" cried Jo.

"Nor I," echoed the others.

"Mother, did you go away just to see how we would get on?" said Meg.

"Yes. I wanted you to see how the comfort of all depends on each doing her share faithfully. I thought I would show you what happens when everyone thinks only of themselves. Isn't it better to help one another, to have regular hours for work and play, and to make each day both useful and pleasant?"

And everyone agreed that it was.

# Chapter 10

# Camp Laurence and Castles in the Air

ONE day, Jo received a note from Laurie:

*Dear Jo,*

*Some English girls and boys are coming to see me tomorrow and I want to have a jolly time. If it's fine, I'm going to pitch my tent in Longmeadow, and row up the whole crew for lunch and croquet. They are nice people. Brooke will go, and Kate Vaughn. I want you all to come.*

*In a tearing hurry, Yours ever,*
*Laurie*

"I hope the Vaughns are not fine, grown-up people," said Meg. "Do you know anything about them, Jo?"

"Only that there are four of them," said Jo. "Kate is older than you, Fred and Frank are twins and about my age, and the little girl, Grace, is nine or ten. You'll come, Beth?"

"If you won't let any of the boys talk to me," said Beth.

"Not a boy!"

The next morning was sunny and Beth gave a running report about what was happening next door whilst her sisters got ready.

"There goes the man with the tent! Mrs Barker is putting the lunch in a hamper. Mr Laurence is looking up at the sky. I wish he would go too. There's Laurie, looking like a sailor! Oh, and here's a carriage full of people – a tall lady, a little girl, and two

dreadful boys. One is lame, poor thing. He's got a crutch. Laurie didn't tell us that. Quick, girls, it's getting late. Look, Meg, isn't that Ned Moffat?"

"So it is," said Meg. "How strange he should come. There's Sallie."

The bright little band of sisters went down to meet Laurie, who presented them to his friends. Tents, lunch and croquet implements had been sent on beforehand, and the party set off in two boats, leaving old Mr Laurence waving his hat on the shore.

Laurie and Jo rowed one boat, Mr Brooke and Ned the other. Kate looked rather amazed when Jo dropped her oar and exclaimed, "Christopher Columbus!" and when Laurie said, "My dear fellow, did I hurt you?" after tripping over Jo's feet, trying to take his place. She came to the conclusion that Jo was 'odd, but rather clever'.

In the other boat, the two young rowers were delighted to be sitting opposite Meg. Mr Brooke was a silent young man, with handsome brown eyes and a pleasant voice. Meg liked his quiet manners and thought him a walking encyclopaedia. Ned was not very wise but good-natured and merry.

It was not far to Longmeadow, but the tent was pitched and the croquet wickets down by the time they arrived.

"Welcome to Camp Laurence!" said Laurie as they landed. "Brooke is

commander-in-chief, I am commissary general, the other fellows are staff officers and you, ladies, are company. Now, let's have a game before it gets hot, then we'll see about some dinner."

Frank, Beth, Amy and Grace sat down to watch the game played by the other eight. Mr Brooke chose Meg, Kate and Fred. Laurie took Sallie, Jo and Ned. The croquet game began and there was some argument between Jo and Fred, particularly when Jo saw him cheat. But she held her temper and, afterwards, Meg congratulated her for doing so.

"Time for lunch," Mr Brooke said after the game was over. "Who can make good coffee?"

"Jo can!" said Meg.

So Jo presided over the coffee-pot while the children collected sticks and the boys made a fire. Miss Kate sketched and Frank talked to Beth, who was making little mats from braided rushes to serve as plates.

It was a merry lunch, and frequent shouts of laughter startled an old horse who was feeding nearby. Afterwards, they sat under a large oak tree and played 'Rigmarole', a story game, then Ned, Frank and the little girls played 'Authors' with Jo and Laurie. The three elders sat apart, talking, and Miss Kate took out her sketch-pad again, and Meg watched her while Mr Brooke lay on the grass with a book he didn't read.

"I wish I could draw," said Meg.

"Why don't you learn?" replied Miss Kate.

"I haven't time."

"Can't your governess – ?"

"I have none," said Meg.

"I forgot that young ladies in America go to school more than us. You go to a private one, I suppose."

"I don't go at all," said Meg. "I'm a governess myself."

"Oh, indeed!" said Miss Kate, but she might as well have said 'How dreadful!' for her tone implied it. Meg's face coloured up.

Mr Brooke said quickly, "Young ladies in America love independence, and are admired and respected for supporting themselves."

Miss Kate shut up her sketch-book. "I must look after Grace, she is romping," she said. Then added to herself, "I didn't come to chaperone a governess, though she *is* young and pretty."

"I forgot that English people rather turn up their noses at governesses," said Meg, frowning as Miss Kate walked away.

"Tutors also have a hard time of it there," said Mr Brooke. "There's no place like America for us workers, Miss Meg."

"I only wish I liked teaching as you do," she said.

"I think you would if you had Laurie for a pupil," said Mr Brooke. "I shall be sorry to lose him next year."

"Off to college, I suppose?" she said.

"Yes, he's nearly ready. And then I shall turn soldier."

"I am glad!" said Meg. "I should think every young man would want to go, even though it's hard for mothers and sisters who stay at home."

"I have neither, and very few friends to care whether I live or die," said Mr Brooke, rather bitterly.

"Laurie and his grandfather would care, and we would be very sorry to have anything happen to you," said Meg.

"Thank you," began Mr Brooke, looking cheerful again. But then Ned came lumbering up on the old horse and there was no more quiet that day.

At sunset, the boats were loaded and the whole party floated down river, singing at the tops of their voices. Later, as the four girls went home through the garden, Miss Kate looked after them, saying, "In spite of their manners, American girls are very nice when one knows them."

"I quite agree with you," said Mr Brooke.

Laurie lay swinging to and fro in his hammock one warm September afternoon when he saw the Marches coming out, as if bound on some expedition. 'What are those girls about now?' he thought.

Each wore a large, flapping hat, a brown linen bag slung over one shoulder, and carried a long stick. Meg had a cushion, Jo a book, Beth a basket and Amy a portfolio. All began to climb the hill that lay between the house and the river.

"That's cool!" said Laurie. "Fancy having a picnic and not asking me. They can't be going in the boat because they haven't got the key. Perhaps they forgot it. I'll take it to them and see what's going on."

Laurie waited at the boat-house, but when they didn't come, he went up the hill. A group of pine trees covered one part of the hill and it was here, by peeking through the bushes, that he found them.

The sisters sat together with sun and shadow flickering over them, the wind lifting their hair and cooling their hot cheeks. Meg sat upon her cushion, sewing daintily and looking as fresh as a rose in her pink dress. Beth was sorting pine cones, for she made pretty things out of them. Amy was sketching a group of ferns, and Jo was knitting as she read aloud.

The boy watched them, feeling that he ought to go as he had not been invited, yet lingering because home seemed lonely. Then Beth saw his wistful face and beckoned him with a smile.

"May I come, or shall I be a bother?" he said.

Meg lifted her eyebrows, but Jo scowled at her and said, "Of course you may."

"If Meg doesn't want me, I'll go away," said Laurie.

"I don't mind," said Meg, "if you do something. It's against the rules to be idle here."

"Finish this story," said Jo, handing him the book.

"Yes'm," was the meek answer.

The story was not a long one, and when he had finished reading it to them, Laurie asked, "And may I ask if this 'society' is a new one?"

"Shall we tell him?" asked Meg.

"He'll laugh," warned Amy.

"Who cares?" said Jo.

"I guess he'll like it," added Beth.

"Of course I shall!" said Laurie. "And I won't laugh. Tell away, Jo, and don't be afraid."

"The idea of being afraid of you! We used

to play *Pilgrim's Progress*, and we've been going on with it all Winter and Summer, trying to work at various tasks. Now the vacation is nearly over and we're glad we didn't waste it."

"Yes, I should think so," said Laurie, thinking regretfully of his own idle days.

"For the fun of it," went on Jo, "we play pilgrims – bring our things in these bags, wear these old hats, use poles to climb the hill – and we call this 'Delectable Mountain', for we can look far away and see the country where we hope to live some time."

Jo pointed, and Laurie looked through an opening in the wood, across the wide blue river, the meadows on the other side, far over the outskirts of the city, to the green hills that rose to meet the sky. The sun was low and the heavens glowed with the splendour of an Autumn sunset.

"Wouldn't it be fun if all the castles in the air which we make could come true, and we could live in them?" said Jo.

"I've made so many it would be hard to choose," said Laurie.

"What's your favourite?" asked Meg.

"If I tell mine, will you tell yours?"

"Yes," they replied.

"After I'd seen the world, I'd settle in Germany and have as much music as I choose. I'd be a famous musician and would never be bothered about money or business, but just enjoy myself and live for what I liked. That's my favourite castle. What's yours, Meg?"

"I should like a lovely house, with handsome furniture and heaps of money. I am to be mistress of it, with servants so that I don't need to work. I wouldn't be idle, but do good and make everyone love me dearly."

"Wouldn't you have a master for your castle in the air?" asked Laurie.

"Yes, why not say you'd have a splendid husband and some angelic little children?" said Jo. "You know your castle wouldn't be perfect without them."

"You'd have nothing but horses, inkstands and novels in yours," answered Meg.

"Wouldn't I though!" said Jo. "I'd have a stable full of Arabian horses, rooms piled with books, and I'd write out of a magic inkstand and my works would be as famous as Laurie's music."

"My dream is to stay at home safe with Father and Mother, and take care of the family," said Beth.

"I want to be the best artist in the world!" said Amy.

"We all want to be rich and famous except Beth," said Laurie.

"If we're all alive in ten years time," said Jo, "let's meet and see how many of us have got our wishes."

"Grandfather wants me to be an India merchant, as he was," said Laurie, "but I don't care about tea and silk and spices, and every sort of rubbish his old ships bring. Going to college ought to satisfy him, for if I give him four years, he ought to let me off from the business. But I've got to do as he did, unless I break away and please myself, as my father did."

"Sail away in one of your ships and only come home again when you've tried your own way," advised Jo, whose imagination was fired by such a daring adventure.

"That's not right, Jo," said Meg. "Laurie, you should do as your grandfather wishes. Do your best at college, and when he sees that you try to please him, he won't be unjust with you. You'd never forgive yourself if you left him without his permission. Do your duty and you'll get your reward, as good Mr Brooke has, by being respected and loved."

"What do you know about him?" asked Laurie.

"Only what your grandpa told Mother about him – how he took care of his mother till she died, and now provides for an old woman who nursed his mother; and how he never tells anyone but is as generous and patient and good as can be."

"It's like Grandpa to find out all about Brooke and tell his goodness to others," said Laurie. "Brooke couldn't understand why your mother was so kind to him, asking him over with me. If I ever get my wish, you see what I'll do for Brooke."

"Do something now by not plaguing his life out," said Meg, sharply.

"How do you know I do, Miss?"

"I can tell by his face. If you've been good, he looks satisfied and walks briskly. If you've plagued him he looks sad and walks slowly."

"Well, I like that!" said Laurie. "I see him bow and smile as he passes your window, but I didn't know you passed messages between you."

"We don't. Don't be angry, and don't tell him I said anything! I didn't mean to preach. Please don't be offended."

Laurie squeezed her hand and smiled. "I'm the one to be forgiven. I've been out of sorts all day. I like to have you tell me my faults, and be sisterly, so don't mind if I'm grumpy sometimes."

Soon after, the faint sound of Hannah ringing a bell warned them that they would just have time to get home for supper.

"May I come again?" asked Laurie.

"Yes, if you're good and do your studies," said Meg, smiling.

"I'll try," said Laurie.

That night, when Beth came to play to Mr Laurence in the twilight, Laurie listened from the shadows of the curtains and watched the old man, who sat with his grey head on his hand and thought about the dead child he had loved so much. Remembering the conversation of the afternoon, Laurie said to himself, "I'll let my castle go and stay with the dear old gentleman while he needs me."

# *Secrets*

JO was in the garret, for October days grew chilly and the afternoons were short. For two or three hours, the sun lay warmly at the high window where, seated on the old sofa, she wrote busily, her papers spread out on a trunk before her. She scribbled away until the last page was filled, then signed her name with a flourish and threw down her pen.

"There, I've done my best!" she said. "If it won't suit, I'll have to wait until I can do better."

She read the manuscript carefully, then tied it up with a smart red ribbon. Then, taking another manuscript from an old kitchen tin which she used as a desk, she put both into her pocket and crept quietly downstairs.

She put on her hat and jacket, left the house noiselessly and took a round-about way to the road where she caught a passing omnibus into town. If anyone had been watching her, they would have thought her movements very peculiar for, after getting off the bus, she half-ran to a certain number in a busy street. She went inside, looked up the dirty stairs and, after a minute, suddenly dived into the street and walked away as rapidly as she came. This she did several times, much to the amusement of a young gentleman lounging in the window of the building opposite. But the third time, Jo gave herself a shake, pulled her hat over her eyes, and walked up the stairs, looking

as if she was going to have all her teeth out.

There *was* a dentist's sign, among others, outside the entrance, and the young man went across to wait.

"It's like her to come alone," he said to himself, "but if she has a bad time, she'll need someone to help her home."

Ten minutes later, Jo came running out with a very red face. When she saw the young gentleman she looked anything but pleased.

"Did you have a bad time?" he asked.

"Not very," she replied.

"How many did you have out?"

Jo looked at her friend as if she did not understand him, then began to laugh. "There are two which I want to come out, but I must wait a week," she said.

"What are you laughing at?" said Laurie, looking mystified. "You're up to some mischief, Jo."

"So are you. What were you doing in the billiard saloon?"

"It was a gymnasium and I was taking a fencing lesson."

"I'm glad you were not in the saloon, because I hope you never go to such places," said Jo.

"Are you going to deliver lectures all the way home?" he asked.

"Of course not, why?"

"Because if you are, I'll take a bus," he said. "I'd like to walk with you and tell you something interesting. It's a secret, and if I

tell you, you must tell me yours."

"I haven't got any," began Jo, but stopped suddenly, remembering that she had.

"You know you have, you can't hide anything."

"You'll not say anything at home, will you?" she said.

"Not a word."

"And you won't tease me?"

"I never tease," said Laurie.

"Well, I've left two stories with a newspaper man, and he's going to give me an answer next week," whispered Jo.

"Hooray for Miss March, the celebrated American authoress!" cried Laurie, throwing up his hat and catching it again. "Won't it be fun to see them in print!"

Jo's eyes sparkled. "Now, what's *your* secret."

"I may get into trouble for telling," he said, "but I didn't promise not to. I know where Meg's glove is."

"Is that all?" said Jo, looking disappointed.

"It's quite enough for the present, as you'll agree when I tell you where it is."

"Tell, then."

Laurie whispered three words in Jo's ear.

She stood and stared at him, looking surprised and displeased, then walked on, saying sharply, "How do you know?"

"Saw it."

"Where?"

"Pocket."

"All this time?"

"Yes, isn't it romantic?"

"No, it's horrid," said Jo.

"Don't you like it?"

"Of course I don't. What would Meg say?"

"You're not to tell anyone."

"I didn't promise."

"I trusted you. I thought you'd be pleased."

"At the idea of someone coming to take Meg away? No, thank you."

"You'll feel better about it when someone comes to take you away."

"I'd like to see anyone try it!" cried Jo, fiercely.

"So should I!" said Laurie, chuckling at the idea.

"I don't think secrets agree with me," sighed Jo.

"Race me down this hill and you'll feel better," suggested Laurie.

Jo darted away, soon leaving hat and comb behind her and scattering hair-pins as she ran, but Laurie reached the bottom first. She came panting up behind him, with flying hair and red cheeks.

"I wish I was a horse," puffed Jo, dropping down under a maple tree, "then I could run for miles and not lose my breath. It was fun! But be an angel and go and pick up my things."

Laurie gathered up the lost property and Jo began to tidy her hair, hoping nobody would pass by until she had finished. But someone did pass by and who should it be but Meg, looking particularly lady-like.

"What in the world are you doing here?" Meg asked. "You've been running, haven't you? Jo, when *will* you stop such romping ways?"

"Don't make me grow up yet, Meg," said Jo. "It's hard enough to have you change all of a sudden." She bent her head to hide her trembling lips, for lately she had felt that Meg was fast growing into a woman, and Laurie's secret made her dread the separation which must come sometime, perhaps soon.

Laurie saw Jo's troubled face and asked Meg quickly, "Where have you been calling, looking so fine?"

"At the Gardiners," said Meg. "Sallie has been telling me about Belle Moffat's wedding. It was very splendid, and they've gone to spend the Winter in Paris. How delightful that must be!"

"Do you envy her, Meg?" said Laurie.

"I'm afraid I do."

"I'm glad!" muttered Jo, pulling on her hat.

"Why?" asked Meg, looking surprised.

"Because if you care so much about riches, you'll never go and marry a poor man," said Jo, frowning at Laurie.

"I shan't *go* and marry anyone," said Meg, walking on with great dignity. The others followed, skipping stones, and 'behaving like children', as Meg said to herself, although she might have been tempted to join them if she'd not been wearing her best dress.

For a week or two, Jo behaved strangely. She rushed to the door when the postman rang, was rude to Mr Brooke whenever they met, would sit looking at Meg with a sad face, and Laurie and her made signs to one another until the girls declared they had both lost their senses.

On the second Saturday after Jo had gone secretly into town, Meg caught sight of Laurie chasing Jo all over the garden before finally collapsing with shrieks of laughter and a great flapping of newspapers.

"What shall we do with that girl?" said Meg. "She never *will* behave like a young lady."

Minutes later, Jo bounced in, sat on a sofa and pretended to read.

"Have you anything interesting there?" asked Meg.

"Only a story," said Jo.

"You'd better read it aloud," said Amy in her most grown-up tone. "That will amuse

us and keep you out of mischief."

Jo began to read very fast. The girls listened with interest, for the tale was romantic and most of the characters died in the end.

Meg wiped away a tear. "I like the loving part," she said. "Viola and Angelo are two of our favourite names. Isn't that strange?"

"Who wrote it?" asked Beth, who had caught the look on Jo's face.

Jo put down the newspaper, and with red cheeks and excitement in her voice replied, "Your sister."

"You?" cried Meg.

"It's very good," said Amy.

"I knew it! Oh, Jo, I *am* so proud!" said Beth, running to hug her sister.

How delighted they all were, although Meg wouldn't believe it until she saw the words, 'Miss Josephine March' printed in the paper. And they were full of questions.

"When did it come?"

"How much did you get for it?"

"What will Father say?"

"Won't Laurie laugh!"

"Stop jabbering and I'll tell you everything," laughed Jo, and told them how she had taken the stories to the newspaper office. "When I went to get my answer, the man said he liked them both but didn't pay beginners. But it was good practise, he said, and when beginners improved, anyone would pay. Oh, I *am* so happy, for in time I may be able to support myself and help the girls."

Jo's breath ran out and she shed a few happy tears, for to be independent, and earn the praise of those she loved, were the dearest wishes of her heart, and this was the first step towards that happy end.

# Chapter 12

# A Telegram

"NOVEMBER is the most disagreeable month in the whole year," said Meg, standing at the window one dull afternoon and looking out at the frost-bitten garden.

"That's the reason I was born in it," said Jo.

"If something very pleasant happened now, we'd think it a delightful month," said Beth.

"I dare say, but nothing pleasant ever *does* happen in this family," said Meg, who was in a bad temper.

"Two pleasant things are going to happen right away," said Beth, looking out of the other window. "Marmee is coming down the street, and Laurie is tramping through the garden as if he had something nice to tell."

In they both came, Mrs March with her usual question, "Any letter from Father, girls?" and Laurie to say, "Won't some of you come for a drive?"

But a sharp ring interrupted them and after a moment Hannah came in.

"It's one of them horrid telegraph things," she said, handling it as if it might explode.

At the word 'telegraph', Mrs March snatched it, read the two lines it contained, and dropped back into her chair as white as if the little paper had sent a bullet to her heart. Laurie dashed downstairs for water while Meg and Hannah supported her, and Jo read aloud in a frightened voice –

"'Mrs March:
*Your husband is very ill. Come at once.*
S. Hale.
Blank Hospital, Washington.'"

How still the room became as they listened. The girls gathered about their mother, feeling as if all the happiness and support of their lives was about to be taken from them.

"I shall go at once," said Mrs March, "but it may be too late. Oh, children, help me to bear it!"

For several minutes, there was nothing but the sound of sobbing. Then Hannah said, "The Lord keep the dear man! I'll get your things ready right away, mum."

They tried to be calm as their mother sat up, looking pale but steady.

"Where's Laurie?" she asked.

"Here, ma'am," cried the boy. "Oh, let me do something!"

"Send a telegram saying I will come at once. The next train goes early in the morning. Leave a note at Aunt March's. Jo, give me that pen and paper."

Jo did as she was asked, knowing that the money for the long journey must be borrowed and feeling as if she would do anything to add a little to the sum for her father.

"Now go, dear," Mrs March said to Laurie, "but don't kill yourself driving at a desperate pace, there's no need for that."

But minutes later, Laurie raced by the window on his horse.

"Jo, run and tell Mrs King I can't come. On the way, get these things. I must go prepared for nursing. Beth, go and ask Mr Laurence for a couple of bottles of old wine. I'm not too proud to beg for Father. Amy, tell Hannah to get down the black trunk, and Meg, come and help me find my things for I'm half bewildered."

Everyone scattered like leaves before a gust of wind, and the quiet, happy household was broken up as if the telegram had been an evil spell.

Mr Laurence came hurrying back with Beth, bringing every comfort he could think of and promising to protect the girls while their mother was away. He offered himself as an escort but Mrs March would not hear of the old gentleman undertaking the long journey, although it was clear she would have like some company. The old man noticed this and marched away, saying he'd be back soon.

No one had time to think of him again until Meg saw Mr Brooke in the doorway.

"I'm very sorry to hear of this, Miss March," he said in a kind, quiet voice. "I came to offer myself as escort to your mother."

"How kind you all are!" said Meg, her face full of gratitude. "It will be such a relief to know she has someone to take care of her. Thank you very, very much!"

Everything was arranged by the time Laurie returned with a note from Aunt March, enclosing the money. The short afternoon wore away, but still Jo did not come and they began to get anxious. Laurie went off to find her, but he missed her and she came walking in and gave a roll of banknotes to her mother.

"That's from me, to help towards making Father comfortable and bringing him home," she said.

"Twenty-five dollars! My dear, where did you get it?"

"I only sold what was my own," said Jo.

As she spoke, she took off her bonnet, and there was a gasp from the others. All her long hair had been cut short.

"Your hair, your beautiful hair!"

"Jo, how could you?"

"My dear girl, there was no need for this."

"She doesn't look like my Jo any more, but I love her dearly for it."

Beth hugged the cropped head tenderly, but Jo said, "Don't wail, Beth. It will do my brains good to have that mop taken off, and the barber said I'd soon have a curly crop which will be boyish and easy to keep in order. So please take the money, Marmee, and let's have supper."

"What made you do it?" said Amy, who

would as soon have thought of cutting off her head as her pretty hair.

"I was wild to do something for Father," said Jo. "Then I saw tails of hair in a barber's window. One black tail, not so thick as mine, was forty dollars. So I walked in and asked if they bought hair, and what they would give me for mine. The barber was startled at first, but I begged him to take it and told him why. His wife overheard and told him to do it. She had a son who was in the army and said she'd do as much for him any day if she had hair worth selling. She picked out a lock from mine when it was cut and gave it to me. I'll give it to you, Marmee, just to remember past glories by."

Much later, when Amy and Beth were asleep and Meg was lying awake, thinking serious thoughts, she heard a sob from Jo's bed. "Jo, dear, what is it?" she asked. "Are you crying for Father?"

"No, my hair," cried Jo, trying to smother her tears in the pillow. "I'd do it again tomorrow, if I could. It's only the vain, selfish part of me that goes and cries in this silly way. Don't tell anyone, it's all over now. How did you come to be awake?"

"I can't sleep," said Meg. "I'm so anxious."

"Think of something pleasant."

"I tried, but I felt wider awake than ever."

"What did you think of?"

"Handsome faces," said Meg, smiling to herself. "Eyes particularly."

"What colour do you like best?"

"Brown – that is, sometimes. Blue are lovely."

Jo laughed, and Meg sharply ordered her not to talk, then fell asleep to dream of living in her castle in the air.

In the cold grey dawn, the sisters lit their lamp and read their chapter with an earnestness never felt before. Everything seemed strange when they went down, so dim and still outside, so full of bustle within. The big trunk stood ready in the hall, Mother's cloak and bonnet lay on the sofa, and Mother sat trying to eat, looking pale and worn.

As the time drew near and they sat waiting for the carriage, Mrs March said, "Children, I leave you to Hannah's care and Mr Laurence's protection. Meg, watch over your sisters. Jo, write to me often and be my brave girl. Beth, comfort yourself with your music. And Amy, help all you can and keep happy and safe at home. Hope and keep busy, all of you."

"We will, Mother! We will!"

Laurie and his grandfather came to see Mrs March off, and Mr Brooke looked so strong and sensible and kind that the girls

christened him 'Mr Greatheart' on the spot.

"Goodbye, my darlings!" whispered Mrs March. "God bless and keep us all." And she kissed one dear little face after another.

As the carriage rolled away, the sun came out, and the last thing Mrs March saw as she turned the corner was the four bright faces, and behind them old Mr Laurence, Hannah and Laurie.

"How kind everyone is to us," she said to Mr Brooke.

And so their long journey began.

"I feel as if there has been an earthquake," said Jo, as their neighbours went home to breakfast.

"It seems as if half the house has gone," added Meg, sadly.

"Hope and keep busy, Mother told us," said Jo. "I shall go to Aunt March, as usual."

"I shall go to the Kings, though I'd much rather stay home and attend to things here," said Meg.

"Beth and I can keep house perfectly well," said Amy, importantly.

"Hannah will tell us what to do, and we'll have everything nice when you come home," said Beth.

When Meg and Jo went out to their daily tasks, they looked sorrowfully back at the window where Mother always stood and waved. Mother was gone, but Beth had remembered the little ceremony and was nodding away at them.

"That's so like Beth," said Jo, waving her hat gratefully. "Goodbye, Meggy. I hope the Kings won't be a lot of trouble today."

"And I hope Aunt March won't complain." Meg tried not to smile at the curly head on Jo's shoulders. "Your hair looks very boyish and nice," she told her sister.

"That's my only comfort," said Jo, feeling like a shorn sheep on a wintry day.

News of their father comforted the girls for, though dangerously ill, the care of the best and tenderest of nurses had already done him good. Mr Brooke sent a letter every day and, as head of the family, Meg insisted on reading them. They grew more and more cheering as the weeks passed.

# Chapter 13

# Little Faithful

"MEG, I wish you'd go and see the Hummels," Beth said, ten days after their mother had gone. "You know Mother told us not to forget them."

"I'm too tired to go this afternoon," said Meg, rocking comfortably as she sewed.

"Can't you, Jo?" asked Beth.

"Too stormy for me with my cold." Jo had caught a cold through neglecting to cover her shorn head.

"I thought it was almost well."

"It's well enough for me to go out with Laurie, but not well enough to go to the Hummels," said Jo, laughing but feeling a little ashamed.

"Why don't you go yourself?" asked Meg.

"I have been every day," said Beth, "but the baby is sick and I don't know what to do for it. I think you or Hannah ought to go."

Meg promised she would go tomorrow.

"Ask Hannah for something nice and take it round, Beth. The air will do you good," said Jo. "I'd go, but I want to finish my writing."

"My head aches and I'm tired," said Beth. "I thought maybe some of you would go."

"Amy will be in presently and she'll go," said Meg.

"Well, I'll rest a little and wait for her."

Beth lay down on the sofa and the Hummels were forgotten. An hour passed and Amy did not come. Meg went to her room to try on a new dress and Jo was absorbed in her story.

Hannah was sound asleep in front of the kitchen fire when Beth quietly put on her hood, filled her basket with odds and ends for the poor children and went out into the chilly air. It was late when she came back and no one saw her creep upstairs and shut herself in her mother's room. Half an hour after, Jo went to Mother's room for something and found Beth sitting on the medicine chest looking very grave, with red eyes and a camphor bottle in her hand.

"Christopher Columbus! What's the matter?" cried Jo.

Beth put out a hand to warn her off. "You've had scarlet fever, haven't you?" she said.

"Years ago when Meg did," said Jo. "Why?"

"Then I'll tell you. Oh, Jo, the baby's dead!" cried Beth. "It died on my lap before Mrs Hummel got home from work."

"My poor dear, how dreadful for you! I ought to have gone," said Jo, taking her sister in her arms as she sat in her mother's big chair.

"It wasn't dreadful, Jo, only so sad! It seemed asleep, but all of a sudden it gave a little cry, then lay very still. I knew it was dead."

"What did you do?"

"I just sat and held it until Mrs Hummel came with the doctor. He said it was dead,

and looked at Heinrich and Minna who have got sore throats. 'Scarlet fever, ma'am. You ought to have called me before,' he said crossly. Mrs Hummel told him she was poor and had tried to cure the baby herself. He was kinder then, but it was very sad. He told me to come home and take belladonna right away or I'd have the fever."

"No, you won't!" cried Jo, hugging her close. "If you should be sick, I could never forgive myself."

"Don't be frightened, I shan't have it badly," said Beth. "I looked in Mother's book and saw that it begins with headaches, a sore throat and odd feelings like mine, so I did take some belladonna and I feel better."

"If only Mother was at home," said Jo, seizing the book. She read a page, looked at Beth, felt her head, peeped into her throat, and then said gravely, "I'm afraid you're going to have it, Beth. I'll call Hannah."

"Don't let Amy come," said Beth. "She never had it and I'd hate to give it to her."

Hannah told Jo not to worry, that everyone had scarlet fever and if it was treated right, nobody died, which greatly relieved Jo.

"I'll tell you what we'll do," Hannah said after she had examined Beth. "We'll have Dr Bangs to look at you, dear, then we'll send Amy off to Aunt March's, out of harm's way. One of you girls can stay home and amuse Beth for a day or two."

"I shall," said Jo, decidedly. "It's my fault she's sick. I told Mother I'd do the errands, and I haven't."

"I'll go and tell Amy," said Meg.

But Amy said she would rather have the fever than go to Aunt March. Meg walked out in despair, and it was left to Laurie to persuade Amy.

"I'll come and take you out every day," he said, "and tell you how Beth is."

"Will you take me out in the trotting wagon with Puck?"

"On my honour as a gentleman."

"And come every single day?"

"See if I don't."

"And bring me back the minute Beth is well?"

"The very minute."

"And go to the theatre?"

"A dozen theatres, if we may."

"Well – I guess – I will," said Amy.

Laurie asked Jo and Meg if he should send a telegram to Mrs March.

"I think we ought to tell her if Beth is really ill," said Meg, "but Hannah says we mustn't, for Mother can't leave Father and it would only make them anxious. Beth won't be sick long, and Hannah knows just what to do. But it doesn't seem right to me."

"Suppose you ask Grandfather after the doctor has been," suggested Laurie.

"We will," said Meg. "Jo, go and get Dr Bangs at once."

"Stay where you are, Jo," said Laurie, taking up his cap. "I'm the errand boy here."

Dr Bangs came. He said Beth had symptoms of the fever but thought she would have it lightly. Amy was ordered away at once and given something to ward off the danger. She left with Jo and Laurie.

Aunt March greeted them in her usual way.

"What do you want now?" she asked sharply.

Jo told her story.

"No more than I expected if you're allowed to go poking about among poor folks," said Aunt March. "Amy can stay and make herself useful if she isn't sick, which I've no doubt she will be. Don't cry, child!"

Amy was on the point of crying, but Jo slyly pulled the tail of Aunt March's parrot which caused it to call out, "Bless my boots!" and Amy laughed instead.

# Chapter 14

# Dark Days

BETH did have the fever and was much sicker than anyone but Hannah and the doctor suspected. The girls knew nothing about illness and Mr Laurence was not allowed to see her, so Hannah had everything her own way. Dr Bangs did his best, but left a good deal to the excellent nurse. Meg stayed home, so as not to infect the Kings, and she kept house. She felt a little guilty when she wrote letters to her mother without mentioning Beth's illness. Jo devoted herself to Beth day and night, which was not hard because Beth was very patient and uncomplaining.

But a time came when she did not know the familiar faces around her and called imploringly for her mother. Then Jo grew frightened, Meg begged to be allowed to write the truth, and Hannah said she would think about it but that there was no danger yet. A letter from Washington added to their trouble, for Mr March was worse again and could not think of coming home for a long while.

How dark the days seemed now, how sad and lonely the house. The sisters worked and waited while the shadow of death hovered over the once happy home. It was then that Meg, tears dropping on her work, felt how rich she had been in things more precious than any luxuries money could buy – in love, peace and health, the real blessings of life. It was then that Jo, living in the darkened room with that suffering little sister, learned to see the beauty of Beth's nature, and to recognise Beth's unselfish ambitions – to live for others and to make home a happy place for all who came there. And Amy longed to be at home, that she might work for Beth, feeling that nothing would be too much trouble.

Laurie haunted the house like a restless ghost, and Mr Laurence locked the grand piano because he could not bear to be reminded of the neighbour who used to make the twilight pleasant for him. Everyone missed Beth.

In her quiet hours, Beth was full of anxiety about Jo. She sent loving messages to Amy, and asked them to tell Mother that she would write soon. But then Beth lay for hours, tossing to and fro or sinking into a heavy sleep. Dr Bangs came twice a day, Hannah sat up at night, Meg kept a telegram ready to send off, and Jo never stirred from Beth's side.

The first of December was a wintry day indeed for them. A bitter wind blew, snow fell fast, and the year seemed to be getting ready for its death. When Dr Bangs came that morning, he looked at Beth, held her hot hand for a moment, then said to Hannah, "If Mrs March *can* leave her husband, she'd better be sent for."

Jo snatched up the telegram, threw on some things and rushed out into the storm. She was soon back and, while taking off her cloak, Laurie came in with a letter saying

that Mr March was mending again. Jo read it thankfully, but her face was so full of misery that Laurie said, "What is it? Is Beth worse?"

"I've sent for Mother," Jo told him. "The doctor told us to."

"Oh, Jo! It's not as bad as that?" cried Laurie.

"Yes it is." The tears streamed down Jo's cheeks. "She doesn't know us. She doesn't look like my Beth."

Laurie took her hand and whispered, "I'm here, hold on to me, Jo."

She could not speak but she did 'hold on', and the warm grasp of the friendly hand comforted her. Laurie longed to say something tender and comforting but no words came to him. But then Jo dried her tears and looked up with a grateful face.

"Thank you, Laurie. I'm better now," she said.

"Your mother will be here soon, Jo, and then everything will be all right," he said.

"I'm so glad Father is better," said Jo. "Now she won't feel so bad about leaving him."

Then Laurie smiled a warm smile. "I sent a telegram to your mother yesterday," he said. "And Brooke answered that she'd come at once. She'll be here tonight and everything will be all right!"

He spoke very fast and his face was red with excitement. He had kept it a secret for fear of disappointing the girls or harming Beth.

Jo threw her arms around his neck. "Oh, Laurie! Oh, Mother! I am so glad." She did not cry again, just laughed and trembled and clung to her friend. Laurie, though amazed, patted her back soothingly and followed this up with a shy kiss or two.

Jo pushed him away, breathlessly. "Oh, don't! I didn't mean to, but you were such a dear to go and do it that I couldn't help flying at you."

"I rather liked it!" laughed Laurie, straightening his tie. "I got fidgety, and so did Grandpa. We thought your mother ought to know. She'd never forgive us if Beth – well, if anything happened, you know. Your mother's train is in at two a.m. and I shall go for her. You only have to keep Beth quiet until that blessed lady gets here."

Laurie departed, pleased that he had done the right thing. Meg was delighted by the news, then brooded over the letter while Jo put the sick-room in order. Hannah said that Laurie was an interfering chap, but she forgave him and hoped Mrs March would come right away.

A breath of fresh air seemed to blow through the house, and each time the girls met, their pale faces broke into smiles and they hugged one another, whispering, "Mother's coming! Mother's coming!" Everyone rejoiced except Beth, who lay unconscious, her once-pretty hair scattered in a tangle on the pillow. All day she lay there, only rousing to mutter, 'Water!' with lips so parched that they could barely shape the word. All day, Meg and Jo hovered over her, watching, waiting, hoping, and trusting in God and Mother. And all the day the snow fell, the bitter wind raged, and the hours dragged slowly by. The doctor came to say that some change, for better or worse, would probably take place about midnight, at which time he would return.

Hannah, quite worn out, fell asleep on the sofa at the foot of the bed. Mr Laurence paced up and down in the parlour, while Laurie lay on the rug, pretending to rest.

The girls never forgot that night.

"If God spares Beth, I'll never complain again," whispered Meg.

"If God spares Beth, I'll try to love and serve him all my life," answered Jo.

The clock struck twelve and a change passed over Beth's face. The house was still as death and only the wailing of the wind broke the deep hush. Hannah slept on, and it was the sisters who saw the pale shadow which seemed to fall upon the little bed. An hour went by, and nothing happened except Laurie's quiet departure for the station.

It was past two when Jo heard a movement by the bed. She was standing at the window thinking how dreary the world looked under the snow, but turned quickly and saw Meg kneeling before her mother's chair with her face hidden. A cold and dreadful fear passed over Jo. 'Beth is dead,' she thought, 'and Meg is afraid to tell me.'

She was back at the bed in an instant – and saw that a great change seemed to have taken place. The fever-flush and the look of pain were gone, and the beloved little face looked so pale and peaceful. Leaning low over this dearest of her sisters, Jo kissed the damp forehead and softly whispered, "Goodbye, my Beth, goodbye!"

Hannah woke up and hurried to the bed. She looked at Beth, felt her hands, listened at her lips, and then, throwing her apron over her head, sat down to rock to and fro. "The fever's turned! She's sleeping natural, her skin's damp and she breathes easy! Praise be given! Oh, my goodness me!"

Before the girls could believe the happy truth, the doctor came to confirm it. "Yes, my dears, I think the little girl will pull through. Keep the house quiet, let her sleep, and when she wakes give – "

What they were to give, neither heard. They crept into the hall and, sitting on the stairs, held each other close, their hearts too full for words. When they went back, they found Beth lying as she used to do, her cheek pillowed on her hand and breathing quietly.

"If Mother would only come now," said Jo.

Never had the sun risen so beautifully, and never had the world seemed so lovely as it did that early morning.

"It looks like a fairy world," said Meg, smiling to herself.

"Hark!" cried Jo.

Yes, there was a sound of bells at the door below, a cry from Hannah, and then Laurie's voice saying in a joyful whisper, "Girls, she's come! She's come!"

# Chapter 15

# Amy's Will

WHILE these things were happening at home, Amy was having a hard time at Aunt March's. For the first time in her life she realised how she was loved and petted at home. Aunt March never petted anyone, but she meant to be kind for the well-behaved little girl pleased her very much, and Aunt March had a soft place in her heart for her nephew's children. She did her best to make Amy happy but, dear me, what mistakes she made! She worried Amy with her prim ways, and her rules and orders.

Amy had to wash the cups every morning, and polish the old-fashioned spoons, the fat silver tea-pot and the glasses until they shone. Then she had to dust the room, and not a speck of dust escaped Aunt March's eye. Then the parrot had to be fed, the lap-dog combed, and a dozen trips made upstairs and down to get things or deliver orders, for the old lady seldom left her big chair. After this, Beth had her lessons to do before being allowed one hour for exercise or play.

And didn't she enjoy that hour! Laurie came every day and persuaded Aunt March to allow Amy to go out with him. They walked and rode and had splendid times. After dinner, she had to read aloud and sit while the old lady slept. Then Amy sewed until dusk, when she was permitted to amuse herself as she liked until tea-time.

She was allowed to roam the house and examine the curious and pretty things stored away in the big wardrobes and ancient chests. Aunt March hoarded like a magpie, and Amy's chief delight was an Indian cabinet full of little drawers, like pigeon holes, and secret places in which were kept all sorts of ornaments and jewellery.

"I wish I knew where all these pretty things will go when Aunt March dies," said Amy.

"To you and your sisters," said Estelle, a French woman who had lived with Aunt March for many years. "I know it because I witnessed her will."

"How nice!" said Amy. "But I wish she'd let us have them now."

"It is too soon yet for the young ladies to wear these things. The first one to be married will have the pearls, Madame has said so. And I fancy the little turquoise ring will be given to you when you go, for Madame approves of your good behaviour and charming manners."

"Do you think so? Oh, I'll be a lamb if only I can have that lovely ring. It's much prettier than Kitty Bryant's. I do like Aunt March after all." And Amy tried on the blue ring with delight.

From that day, Amy was the model of obedience. And she tried to forget herself, to keep cheerful, and to be satisfied with doing right. In her first effort at being good, she decided to make a will as Aunt March had

done. During one of her play hours, she wrote out the important document and, when the good-natured French woman had signed her name, put it to one side to show Laurie whom she wanted as a second witness.

As it was a rainy day, she went upstairs to amuse herself. In one room there was a wardrobe full of old-fashioned costumes, and it was her favourite game to dress up in the faded clothes and parade in front of the long mirror, making stately curtsies and sweeping her train about with a rustle that delighted her ears.

She was so busy on this day that she did not hear Laurie's ring, nor see his face peeping in at her as she promenaded to and fro, waving her fan and tossing her head, on which she wore a great pink turban. Trying not to laugh, Laurie tapped the door.

"Sit down while I put these things away," said Amy, her face red. "I want to talk to you about a very serious matter." She put the clothes back into the wardrobe and shut the doors, then she took a piece of paper from her pocket. "I want you to read that, please, and tell me if it's legal and right. I think I ought to do it because life is uncertain."

Laurie hid a smile and read the document. It said:

*MY LAST WILL AND TESTAMENT*
*I, Amy Curtis March do give my property to the following people.*
*To my father, my best sketches, maps and works of art, including frames. Also my $100 to do what he likes with.*

*To my mother, all my clothes, except the blue apron with pockets. Also my medal, with much love.*

*To my dear sister Meg, I give my turquoise ring (if I get it), also my green box with doves on it, also my piece of real lace for her neck, and my sketch of her as a little girl.*

*To Jo I leave my breast-pin, the one mended with sealing wax, also my bronze ink-stand – she lost the cover – and my precious plaster rabbit because I'm sorry I burnt her story.*

*To Beth (if she lives after me) I give my dolls, my fan, my linen collars, and my new slippers if she can wear them when she gets well.*

*To my friend and neighbour, Theodore Laurence, I give my clay model of a horse, even though he said it had no neck, and any one of my artistic works he likes best.*

*To old Mr Laurence, I leave my purple box which will be nice for his pens and remind him of the departed girl who thanks him for his favours to her family, especially Beth.*

*I wish my favourite playmate, Kitty Bryant, to have the blue silk apron and my gold bead ring with a kiss.*

*To Hannah I give the bandbox she wanted and all the patchwork I leave.*

*To this will and testament I set my hand on this 20th day of November, 1861.*

*AMY CURTIS MARCH*
*Witnesses: Estelle Valnor*
*Theodore Laurence*

The last name was written in pencil and Amy explained that he was to write it in ink and seal it up for her properly.

"What put it into your head?" asked Laurie. "Did anyone tell you about Beth giving away her things?"

She explained, then asked anxiously, "What about Beth?"

"She felt so ill one day that she wanted to give her piano to Meg, her cats to you, and the poor old doll to Jo, who would love it for her sake. She was sorry she had so little to give, and left locks of hair to the rest of us, and her best love to Grandpa. *She* never thought of a will."

Amy's face was full of trouble. "Don't people put sort of postscripts to their wills sometimes?" she said.

"Yes," said Laurie. "They call them codicils."

"Put one in mine then – that I wish *all* my curls cut off and given round to my friends."

Laurie added it, smiling at Amy's last and greatest sacrifice. Then he amused her for an hour. But when he came to go, Amy held him back with a whisper, "Is there really any danger about Beth?"

"I'm afraid there is," said Laurie. "But we must hope for the best." And he put an arm around her, which was very comforting.

When he had gone, Amy prayed for Beth with tears streaming and her heart aching. She felt that a million turquoise rings would not console her for the loss of her gentle little sister.

# Chapter 16

# Confidential

WHEN Beth woke from her long, healing sleep, the first thing she saw was her mother's face. Too weak to wonder at anything, she only smiled and nestled into the arms about her. Then she slept again and the girls waited on their mother, for Mrs March would not let go of the thin hand which clung to hers even in sleep. Hannah had made breakfast for the traveller, and Meg and Jo fed their mother whilst listening to an account of their father's health, Mr Brooke's promise to stay and nurse him, the delays caused by the storm on the journey home, and the comfort Laurie's hopeful face had given her when she'd arrived, tired and cold.

What a strange yet pleasant day that was. Meg and Jo closed their weary eyes and rested at last. Mrs March would not leave Beth's side but rested in the big chair.

Laurie hurried off to comfort Amy, and told his story so well that Aunt March never once said 'I told you so'. Amy dried her tears quickly and restrained her impatience to see her mother. Laurie was dropping with sleep and she persuaded him to rest on the sofa while she went to write a note to Mrs March. When she returned, he was sound asleep.

After a while, they began to think he was not going to wake until night, and indeed he might not had he not been roused by Amy's cry of joy at the sight of her mother coming up the path of Aunt March's house.

There were probably a good many happy little girls in and about the city that day, but Amy was the happiest of all as she sat in her mother's lap.

"I've thought a great deal lately about my 'bundle of naughties', and being selfish is the largest one in it," said Amy. "Beth isn't selfish, and that's the reason everyone loves her. People wouldn't feel half so bad about me if I was sick, but I'd like to be loved and missed by a great many friends, so I'm going to try and be like Beth all I can."

Her mother hugged her. "I think you will succeed, my dear, for the wish to be good is half the battle. Now I must go back to Beth. Keep up your heart, little daughter, and we'll soon have you home again."

That evening, while Meg was writing to her father to report her mother's safe arrival, Jo slipped upstairs to Beth's room and, finding her mother in her usual place, hesitated a minute, twisting her hair in her fingers.

"What is it, dear?" asked Mrs March, holding out her hand.

"I want to tell you something, Mother."

"About Meg?"

"How quickly you guessed! Yes, it's about her."

"Beth is asleep. Speak low and tell me all about it."

"Last Summer, Meg left a pair of gloves over at the Laurences' and only one was returned," said Jo. "We forgot all about it until Laurie told me that Mr Brooke had it.

He kept it in his waistcoat pocket, and once it fell out and Laurie teased him about it. Mr Brooke admitted that he liked Meg but didn't dare say so, she was so young and he was so poor. Now isn't that a *dreadful* state of things?"

"Do you think Meg cares for him?" asked Mrs March, with an anxious look.

"Mercy me! I don't know anything about love!" cried Jo. "In novels, girls show it by blushing, fainting, growing thin and acting like fools. Now Meg doesn't do anything of the sort. She eats, drinks and sleeps like a sensible creature. She looks straight in my face when I talk about that man, and only blushes a little when Laurie jokes about lovers."

"Then you think Meg is *not* interested in John?"

"Who?"

"Mr Brooke. I call him John now, since our time at the hospital."

"Oh dear, I know he's been good to Father and that you'll let Meg marry him if she wants to. Mean thing! To go petting Pa and making up to you, just to wheedle you into liking him!" said Jo.

"My dear, don't get angry. John went with me because Mr Laurence asked him to, and he was so devoted to Father that we couldn't help getting fond of him. He was perfectly open and honourable about Meg and told us that he loved her, but would earn a comfortable home before he asked her to marry him. He only wanted our permission to love her and work for her, and the right to make her love him if he could. He's an excellent young man, but I will not consent to Meg getting engaged so young."

"I knew there was mischief brewing!" said Jo. "But it's worse than I imagined. I wish I could marry Meg myself and keep her safe in the family!"

This made Mrs March smile, but she said seriously, "Jo, I don't want you to say anything to Meg yet. When John comes back and I see them together, I shall be able to judge her feelings towards him."

"She'll look in those handsome eyes that she talks about and then she'll go and fall in love with him. He'll scratch up a fortune somehow, carry her off, and there will be an end of peace and fun and cosy times together. Oh, why weren't we all boys, then there wouldn't be any bother."

"Your Father and I have agreed that she should not be married before twenty," said Mrs March. "She's seventeen now, and if she and John love one another they can wait, and test their love by doing so."

"Wouldn't you rather she married a rich man?" asked Jo.

"Money is a good and useful thing, Jo," said Mrs March, "and I hope my girls will never need it too badly or be tempted by too much. I should like to know that John had an income large enough to keep free from debt and make Meg comfortable, but I'm not ambitious for a fortune or a great name for my girls. I know by experience how much genuine happiness can be had in a plain little house where some hardships make a few pleasures even sweeter. I'm content to see Meg begin humbly for, if I'm not mistaken, she'll have a good man's heart, and that is better than a fortune."

"I understand, Mother," said Jo. "But I'm disappointed about Meg for I'd planned to have her marry Laurie by-and-by, and sit in the lap of luxury all her days."

"I'm afraid Laurie is hardly grown-up enough for Meg," said her mother. "Don't make plans, Jo. Let time and their own hearts bring your friends together."

Jo sighed. "I wish wearing flat-irons on our heads would keep us from growing up," she said. "But buds will be roses and kittens will be cats, more's the pity!"

"What's all this about flat-irons and cats?" asked Meg, as she crept into the room, with the letter to her father in her hand.

"Only one of my stupid speeches," said Jo. "Come on, Meggy, I'm going to bed."

Mrs March glanced over the letter. "Quite right and beautifully written," she said to Meg. "Please add that I send my love to John."

"Do you call him John?" asked Meg, smiling, her innocent eyes looking into her mother's.

"Yes, he's been like a son to us, and we are very fond of him," replied Mrs March, returning the look with a keen one.

"I'm glad of that, he is so lonely," was Meg's quiet answer. "Goodnight, Mother dear."

The kiss her mother gave her was a very tender one. As she went away, Mrs March said with a mixture of satisfaction and regret, "She does not love John yet, but will soon learn to."

# Chapter 17

# Laurie Makes Mischief and Jo Makes Peace

THE secret weighed heavy on Jo, and next day she found it hard not to look mysterious. Meg noticed this but knew that the best way to deal with Jo, and to be certain of knowing everything, was not to ask. Meg was surprised, therefore, when the silence went on. It irritated her and she decided to ignore Jo and devote her time to her mother, who had taken Jo's place as nurse.

With Amy gone, Laurie was Jo's only company, although she was afraid he would coax her secret from her. And she was right, for the mischief-loving lad no sooner suspected a mystery than he set about finding it out. He wheedled, bribed, threatened and scolded until he satisfied himself that it concerned Meg and Mr Brooke. Feeling cross that his tutor had said nothing, Laurie then set his mind to working out some kind of revenge.

Meg meanwhile had apparently forgotten the matter and was busy with preparations for her father's return. But all of a sudden a change seemed to come over her and, for a day or two, she was quite unlike herself. She jumped when spoken to, blushed when looked at, was very quiet and sat over her sewing with a troubled look on her face. To her mother's questions she answered that she was quite well. Jo's she silenced by begging to be left alone.

"She's got most of the symptoms of love," Jo said to her mother, looking ready to do anything, however violent. "She's twittery and cross, doesn't eat, lies awake, and mopes in corners. And once she said 'John' as you do, and then turned red as a poppy. Whatever shall we do?"

"Wait," said her mother. "Be kind and patient."

The next day, a note arrived for Meg. Mrs March and Jo were busy with their own affairs when a sound from Meg made them look up to see her staring at her note with a frightened face.

"My child, what is it?" cried her mother.

"It's all a mistake – he didn't send it. Oh, Jo, how could you do it?" Meg hid her face in her hands and cried as if her heart was broken.

"Me? I've done nothing!" said Jo, bewildered.

Meg pulled another, crumpled note from her pocket and threw it at Jo.

"You wrote it and that bad boy helped you. How could you be so mean and cruel to us both?"

Jo and her mother read the note. It was written in a peculiar handwriting.

*MY DEAREST MARGARET, I can no longer hide my passion and must know my fate before I return. I dare not tell your parents yet, but I think they would consent if they knew that we adore one another. Mr Laurence will help me to find a good place, and then, my sweet girl, you will make me happy. I beg you to say nothing to*

*your family yet, but to send one word of hope through Laurie to*

*Your devoted JOHN*

"Oh, the little villain!" cried Jo. "He's done this because I kept my word to Mother and said nothing. I'll give him a scolding and bring him over to say sorry."

But her mother held her back. "Stop, Jo. You've played so many pranks that I'm afraid you've had a hand in this."

"On my word, Mother, I haven't!" said Jo. "I never saw that note before. If I *had* taken part in it, I'd have done it better and written a sensible note. Mr Brooke wouldn't write such stuff as that."

"It's like his writing," said Meg, comparing the note in her hand.

"Oh, Meg, you didn't answer it?" cried Mrs March quickly.

"Yes, I did!" Meg hid her face again, overcome with shame.

Mrs March sat down beside her. "Tell me the whole story, Meg."

"Laurie brought the first letter, looking as if he knew nothing about it," began Meg. "I was worried at first, and meant to tell you. Then I remembered how you liked Mr Brooke, so I thought you wouldn't mind if I kept my little secret for a few days. Forgive me, Mother. I can never look him in the face again."

"What did you say to him?" asked Mrs March.

"I only said that I was too young to do anything about it yet, and that I didn't wish to have secrets from you so he must speak to Father. I said I would be his friend, but nothing more for a long while."

Mrs March smiled, as if well-pleased, and Jo clapped her hands and laughed.

"What did he say to that, Meg?" she asked.

"He wrote saying that he never sent any love letter at all, and is very sorry my roguish sister Jo should play such a trick. It's a very kind and respectful note, but think how dreadful for me."

"I don't believe Brooke ever saw either of these letters," said Jo. "Laurie wrote them both and he's keeping yours to crow about because I wouldn't tell him my secret."

"That will do, Jo," said Mrs March. "I'll comfort Meg while you go and get Laurie. I'll put a stop to such pranks at once."

Away ran Jo, and Mrs March gently told Meg Mr Brooke's real feelings. "Now dear, what are your own? Do you love him enough to wait until he can make a home for you, or will you keep yourself free for the present?"

"I've been so scared and worried, I don't want anything to do with love for a long while – perhaps never," answered Meg. "If

John *doesn't* know anything about this nonsense, don't tell him, and make Jo and Laurie hold their tongues. I won't be made a fool of!"

Mrs March soothed her daughter's anger, but the instant Laurie's step was heard in the hall, Meg fled into the study and Mrs March saw the culprit alone. Jo had not told him why he was wanted, but Laurie knew the minute he saw Mrs March's face. Jo waited outside, marching up and down the hall. The voices in the parlour rose and fell for half an hour, but what happened during that interview, the girls never knew.

When they were called in, Laurie was standing by their mother with such a sorrowful face that Jo forgave him instantly, but did not say so. He humbly apologised to Meg, who was relieved to hear that Brooke knew nothing of the joke.

"I'll never tell him," said Laurie, looking very ashamed of himself. "Please forgive me, Meg."

"I'll try, but I didn't think you could be so unkind," said Meg.

"I don't deserve to be spoken to for a month," said Laurie, "but you will though, won't you?" He said it in such a persuasive way that Meg forgave him and Mrs March's serious face relaxed.

Jo, however, tried to harden her heart and look annoyed. Laurie glanced at her once or twice but, seeing that she showed no sign of softening, eventually bowed to her and walked off without a word.

As soon as he'd gone, Jo wished she had been more forgiving, and when Meg and her mother had gone upstairs she went over to the big house.

"Is Mr Laurence in?" Jo asked a housemaid.

"Yes, miss, but you can't see him."

"Why not? Is he ill?"

"No, miss, but he's had an argument with Mr Laurie, who is in a tantrum about something."

"Where is Laurie?" asked Jo.

"Shut up in his room, and he won't answer. I don't know what's to become of dinner, for it's ready and there's no one to eat it."

"I'll go and see what the matter is," said Jo. "I'm not afraid of either of them."

Jo went upstairs and knocked smartly on the door of Laurie's little study.

"Stop that, or I'll come out and make you!" he called.

Jo pounded again and the door flew open. She bounced in before he could recover from his surprise, then dropped to her knees. "Please forgive me for being so cross," she said. "I've come to make it up."

"It's all right. Get up and don't be a goose, Jo," was the reply.

"Thank you, I will," said Jo. She looked at him. "What's the matter?"

"I've been shaken, and I won't bear it," he growled.

"Who did it?" demanded Jo.

"Grandfather. If it had been anyone else – "

"Why did he do it?"

"Because I wouldn't say what your mother wanted me for. I'd promised not to tell, and I wasn't going to break my word. I put up with the scolding until he collared me, then I got angry and bolted."

"It wasn't nice, but he's sorry, I know he is," said Jo. "Go down and make it up. I'll help you."

"No, I'm not going to be lectured by everyone just for a bit of a joke. I *was* sorry about Meg, and I asked to be forgiven, like a man. But I won't do it again when I wasn't in the wrong. He ought to believe me when I say I can't tell him what the fuss is about. I won't go down until he apologises."

"Now Laurie, be sensible, let it pass and I'll explain what I can."

"I'll slip off and take a journey somewhere, and when Grandpa misses me he'll come round fast enough," said Laurie.

"You mustn't go and worry him," said Jo.

"Don't preach. I'll go to Washington and see Brooke, that's what I'll do."

"What fun you'd have! I wish I could run off, too," said Jo, forgetting for a moment that she was supposed to be giving him sensible advice.

"Come on then! Why not? You go and surprise your Father, and I'll stir up old Brooke. It would be a glorious joke! We'll leave a letter saying we're all right, and go at once."

For a moment Jo looked as if she would agree, but then she glanced out of the window and saw the old house opposite and shook her head.

"If I was a boy, we'd run away together and have a splendid time. But as I'm a miserable girl, I must be proper and stay at home. Don't tempt me, Laurie, it's a crazy plan. Listen, if I get your grandpa to apologise for the shaking, will you give up running away?"

"Yes, but you won't do it," answered Laurie.

"If I can manage the young one, I can the old one," Jo muttered as she walked away.

"Come in!" said Mr Laurence's gruff voice, as Jo tapped his door.

"It's only me, sir, come to return a book," she said.

"Want any more?" asked the old gentleman, looking grim and cross but trying not to show it.

"Yes, please." She went to the bookcase and pretended to be looking for a book.

"What's that boy been doing?" he asked suddenly. "I know he's been in mischief by the way he acted when he came home. I can't get a word out of him, and when I tried to shake the truth from him he ran upstairs."

"He did do wrong and we forgave him," said Jo, "but we all promised not to say a word to anyone."

"That won't do! He'll not hide behind a promise from you soft-hearted girls. Out with it, Jo! I won't be kept in the dark!"

"I can't sir, because Mother has forbidden it," Jo said. Mr Laurence looked so alarming that she would have gladly run away if she could. "We are not keeping silent to shield him but someone else, and it will make trouble if you interfere. Please don't, it was partly my fault but it's all right now."

"Give me your word this boy of mine hasn't done anything ungrateful or rude. If

he has, after all your kindness to him, I'll thrash him with my own hands."

The threat did not alarm Jo for she knew that he would never lift a finger against his grandson. So she made as light of the prank as she could without betraying Meg or forgetting the truth.

"Well, if the boy held his tongue because he'd promised and not from obstinacy, I'll forgive him," said Mr Laurence. "He's a stubborn fellow and hard to manage."

"So am I," said Jo, "but a kind word will always work with me."

"You think I'm not kind to him?"

"Too kind, sometimes,' said Jo, nervously, "but just a little hasty when he tries your patience."

The old gentleman sighed. "You're right, I am. I love the boy but he tries my patience past bearing. I don't know how it will end."

"I'll tell you, he'll run away."

Jo was immediately sorry she'd said that, for Mr Laurence sat down with a troubled glance at a picture of a handsome man which hung over his table. It was Laurie's father, who *had* run away in his youth, and married against the old man's wishes.

"He won't do it unless he's very worried, and only threatens it when he gets tired of studying," said Jo. "I often think I'd like to, especially since my hair was cut. So if you ever miss us you should look for two boys amongst the ships going to India." She smiled as she spoke and Mr Laurence looked relieved, taking the whole thing as a joke.

"Go and bring that boy down," he said, looking a little ashamed of his temper. "Tell him it's all right. I'm sorry I shook him, and ought to thank him for not shaking *me*, I suppose. But what does he expect?"

"I'd write him an apology, sir. He says he won't come down until he has one. A formal apology will make him see how

foolish he is. Try it. He likes fun, and this way is better than talking. I'll take it up."

Mr Laurence gave her a sharp look and put on his spectacles. "Here, give me a bit of paper, and let's have done with this nonsense."

The note was written and Jo dropped a kiss on Mr Laurence's bald head. Then she slipped the note under Laurie's door. She was going quietly away when the young gentleman slid down the banisters and waited for her at the bottom of the stairs.

"What a good fellow you are, Jo," he said. "Did you get blown up?"

"No, he was pretty mild on the whole. Now, go and eat your dinner, you'll both feel better after it." And Jo whisked out of the front door.

Everyone thought the matter was ended, but though others forgot it, Meg remembered. She never talked about a certain person, but she thought of him a good deal and dreamed her dreams. And once, when Jo was looking in her sister's desk for a stamp, she found a bit of paper scribbled over with the words, 'Mrs John Brooke'.

Jo just groaned.

# Pleasant Meadows

THE peaceful weeks that followed were like the sunshine after a storm. Mr March began to talk of returning in the new year, and Beth was soon able to lie on the study sofa all day, amusing herself with her beloved cats. Her limbs were still weak and stiff, so Jo carried her on a daily airing around the house. Meg cheerfully blackened and burned her white hands, cooking delicate things for Beth, and Amy gave away as many of her treasures as her sisters would accept.

Christmas Day promised to be a grand success that year. To begin with, Mr March wrote to say that he would soon be with them. Then Beth felt much better that morning and was carried to the window to see Jo and Laurie's offering. These two had worked by night, and there in the garden stood a snow-maiden, crowned with holly, bearing a basket of fruit and flowers in one hand, a great roll of new music in the other, a rainbow-coloured shawl round her shoulders, and a Christmas carol coming from her mouth on a pink paper streamer!

How Beth laughed when she saw it! Laurie ran up and down to bring in the gifts and Jo made silly speeches as she presented them.

"I'm so full of happiness that, if Father were only here, I couldn't hold one drop more," said Beth, as Jo carried her back to the study to rest after the excitement.

Half an hour later, Laurie opened the parlour door and popped his head in very quietly. He might just as well have turned a somersault and given an Indian war-cry because his face was full of excitement.

"Here's another Christmas present for the March family," he said in a breathless voice.

He was whisked away somehow, and in his place appeared a tall man, muffled up to the eyes, leaning on the arm of another tall man. There was a general stampede, and Mr March became invisible under four pairs of loving arms. Jo nearly fainted and had to be helped by Laurie. Mr Brooke kissed Meg, entirely by mistake as he tried to explain. And the dignified Amy tumbled over a stool and, not stopping to get up, hugged and cried over her father's boots.

Mrs March was the first to recover. "Hush!" she said. "Remember Beth."

But it was too late, for the study door flew open and Beth ran straight into her father's arms.

Mrs March thanked Mr Brooke for his faithful care of her husband, then the young man and Laurie left. Afterwards, the two invalids were ordered to rest, which they did by both sitting in one big armchair and talking.

Mr March told how he had longed to surprise them and how the doctor had allowed him to come. He said how devoted Brooke had been and what an admirable young man he was. He glanced at Meg, who was violently poking the fire, then looked at his wife with an inquiring lift of his eyebrow. Mrs March gently nodded her head. Jo saw and understood the look and she stalked grimly away to get beef-tea, muttering to herself as she slammed the door, "I hate admirable men with brown eyes!"

There never *was* such a Christmas dinner as they had that day. The fat turkey was a sight to behold, and so was the plum pudding, which melted in the mouth. Mr Laurence and his grandson dined with them, as did Mr Brooke. Jo scowled at him darkly, much to Laurie's amusement.

A sleigh-ride had been planned, but the girls would not leave their father. So the guests departed early and, as twilight gathered, the happy family sat together round the fire.

"Just a year ago we were groaning over the dismal Christmas we expected to have. Do you remember?" said Jo.

"It's been rather a pleasant year on the whole!" said Meg, smiling at the fire and thinking of Mr Brooke.

"I think it's been a pretty hard one," said Amy.

"I'm glad it's over, because we've got you back," whispered Beth, who was sitting on her father's knee.

"Rather a rough road for you to travel, my little pilgrims," said Mr March. "But you've got on bravely and your burdens are ready to tumble off very soon."

"How do you know? Did Mother tell you?" asked Jo.

"A little. But I've made several discoveries today."

"Oh, tell us what they are!" cried Meg.

"Here is one," he said, taking her hand and pointing to a burn on the back and two or three little hard spots on the palm. "I remember when this hand was white and smooth and your first care was to keep it so. It was pretty then, but to me it's much prettier now. I'm proud to shake this hard-working hand, Meg, and I hope I'll not be soon asked to give it away."

"What about Jo?" Beth whispered in her father's ear. "She has tried so hard."

Mr March looked across at the tall girl who sat opposite. "In spite of the curly crop, I see a young lady who doesn't whistle, talk slang or lie on the rug any more. Her face is thin and pale from anxiety but I like to look at it because it has grown gentler. She doesn't bounce but moves quietly, and takes care of a certain little person in a motherly way. I rather miss my wild girl, but if I get a strong but tender-hearted woman in her place, I shall feel satisfied."

Jo's face grew rosy in the firelight as she received her father's praise.

"Now Beth," said Amy, longing for her turn but ready to wait.

"She's not as shy as she used to be," said her father, cheerfully, but then he remembered how near they had come to losing her and he held Beth close, her cheek against his own. "I've got you safe, my Beth, and I'll keep you so, please God." After a silent moment or two, he looked down at Amy who sat at his feet. "I noticed that Amy ran errands for her mother, gave Meg her place tonight, and has waited on everyone with patience and good humour. She has learned to think of other people more, and of herself less."

"What are you thinking of, Beth?" asked Jo, when Amy had thanked her father.

"I read in *Pilgrim's Progress* today how, after many troubles, Christian and Hopeful came to a pleasant green meadow, and there they rested happily, as we do now, before they went on to their journey's end," answered Beth. She slipped out of her father's arms and went slowly across to her piano. "It's singing time now and I want to be in my old place. I'll try to sing the song of the shepherd boy which the pilgrims heard. I made the music for Father because he likes the words."

So, sitting at the piano, Beth softly touched the keys and began to sing.

"He that is down need fear no fall,
He that is low no pride;
He that is humble ever shall
Have God to be his guide."

# Chapter 19

# Aunt March Settles the Question

LIKE bees swarming after their queen, mother and daughters hovered around Mr March the next day. As he sat propped up in the big chair by Beth's sofa, nothing seemed needed to complete their happiness. But something *was* needed. Mr and Mrs March looked at one another anxiously as their eyes followed Meg. Jo was seen to shake her fist at Mr Brooke's umbrella which had been left in the hall. Meg was absent-minded, jumped whenever the bell rang, and coloured when John's name was mentioned. As Amy said, everyone seemed to be waiting for something, which was strange now that Father was home. And Beth innocently wondered why their neighbours didn't run over as usual.

Laurie went by in the afternoon and, seeing Meg at the window, fell on one knee in the snow, beat his chest, tore his hair, and clasped his hands imploringly. When Meg told him to go away, he wrung imaginary tears out of his handkerchief and staggered round the corner as if in despair.

"What does the goose mean?" said Meg, laughing.

"He's showing you how your John will act, by-and-by," answered Jo, scornfully.

"Don't say *my John*, it isn't proper or true." But Meg's voice lingered over the words as if they sounded pleasant to her. "There isn't anything to be said. We are all to be friendly and go on as before."

"We can't, for something *has* been said, and Laurie's mischief has spoilt you for me," said Jo. "You're not your old self, and you seem so far away from me. I'll bear it like a man, but I wish it was all settled. If you mean to do it, make haste and have it over quickly."

"*I* can't say or do anything until he speaks, and he won't because Father said I was too young," began Meg, smiling as if she did not quite agree with her father on that point.

"If he did speak you wouldn't know what to say. You'd cry or blush, or let him have his own way instead of giving a decided 'No'."

"I'm not as silly or weak as you think. I should say, quite calmly, 'Thank you, Mr Brooke, you are very kind, but I agree with Father that I am too young to enter into an engagement at present. So please say no more but let us be friends as we were.'"

"I don't believe you'll ever say it. You'll give in rather than hurt his feelings."

"No, I won't. I'll tell him I've made up my mind, then walk out of the room with dignity." Meg rose, as if to rehearse the dignified exit, but a step in the hall made her fly to her seat and begin sewing as if her life depended on it. Jo smothered a laugh and, when a tap came at the door, opened it with a scowl.

"Good afternoon, I came to get my umbrella – that is, to see how your father is

today," said Mr Brooke, getting confused as he looked from one to the other.

"It's very well, he's in the rack, I'll get him and tell it you are here," said Jo, jumbling her father and the umbrella together in her reply. She slipped out of the room to give Meg a chance to make her speech, but the instant she vanished, Meg began to sidle towards the door.

"Mother will like to see you," she murmured. "Please sit down, I'll call her."

"Don't go. Are you afraid of me, Margaret?" Mr Brooke looked hurt, and Meg blushed up to the little curls on her forehead. He had never called her Margaret before.

"How can I be afraid when you have been so kind to Father," she said. "I only wish I could thank you for it."

"Shall I tell you how?" Mr Brooke took Meg's small hand in his and looked down at her with so much love that her heart began to flutter.

"Oh, please don't – I'd rather not," she said, trying to withdraw her hand and looking frightened.

"I only want to know if you care for me a little, Meg," he said tenderly. "I love you so much."

This was the moment for her speech but Meg forgot every word of it. "I don't know," she said, so softly that John had to stoop down to catch her reply.

He smiled and pressed her hand gratefully. "Will you try to find out? I want to know *so* much, for I can't work with any heart until I learn your answer."

"I'm too young," said Meg.

"I'll wait. In the meantime, you could be learning to like me. Would it be a very hard lesson, dear?"

"Not if I choose to learn it."

"Please choose, Meg, I love to teach, and this is easier than German," broke in John, taking her other hand.

She stole a sly look at him and saw that his eyes were merry as well as tender, and that he wore a satisfied smile as if sure of success. This made her cross. Withdrawing her hands, she said, "I *don't* choose. Please go away and let me be!"

Poor Mr Brooke looked as if his lovely castle in the air was tumbling about his ears. "Do you really mean that?"

"Yes, I don't want to be worried about such things. Father says I needn't and I'd rather not."

"May I hope you'll change your mind? I'll wait and say nothing until you've had more time." He looked at her so wistfully, so tenderly, that she found her heart softening in spite of herself.

It was at this very interesting moment that Aunt March came hobbling in. The old lady had heard from Laurie of Mr March's arrival and had driven straight out to the house to see her nephew. The family were all busy at the back of the house and she made her way in quietly, hoping to surprise them. She did surprise two of them, so much that Meg started as if she'd seen a ghost and Mr Brooke vanished into the study.

"Bless me, what's all this?" cried the old lady with a rap of her cane and glancing from the pale young gentleman to the scarlet young lady.

"It's Father's friend," stammered Meg. "I'm *so* surprised to see you, Aunt March."

"That's obvious," said Aunt March, sitting down. "But what is Father's friend saying to make you as red as a peony?"

"We were just talking. Mr Brooke came for his umbrella."

"Brooke? The boy's tutor? Ah! I understand now. I know all about it because Jo blundered into the wrong part of one of your father's letters, and I made her tell me. You haven't gone and accepted him, child?" cried Aunt March, looking scandalised.

"Hush, he'll hear! Shall I call Mother?" said Meg, much troubled.

"Not yet, I've something to say. Do you mean to marry him? If you do, not one penny of my money ever goes to you," said the old lady. "Remember that and be a sensible girl."

If Aunt March had begged Meg to accept John Brooke, Meg would probably have declared that she couldn't do it. But after being ordered *not* to like him, she immediately made up her mind that she would.

"I shall marry whom I please, Aunt March, and you can leave your money to anyone you like."

"Highty-tighty! You'll be sorry!" Aunt March put on her glasses and looked at the girl, for she did not recognise her in this mood. She had begun in the wrong way and, after a moment, made a fresh start. "Meg, my dear, be reasonable and take my advice. You ought to marry well, and help your family. It's your duty to make a rich match."

"Father and Mother don't think so. They like John, even though he's poor."

"He hasn't got a business, has he?"

"Not yet, but Mr Laurence is going to help him."

"That won't last long. James Laurence is a crotchety old fellow, and not to be depended upon. So you intend to marry a man without money, position or business. I thought you had more sense, Meg."

"I couldn't do better if I waited half my life!" said Meg. "John is good and wise, he's got heaps of talent and he's sure to get on. Everyone likes and respects him, and I'm proud to think he cares for me, though I'm so poor and young and silly."

"He knows *you* have rich relations, child. That's why he likes you, I suspect."

"Aunt March, how dare you say such a thing!" cried Meg, forgetting everything but the injustice of her aunt's suspicions. "My John wouldn't marry for money any more than I would. We are willing to work and we mean to wait. I shall be happy with him because he loves me, and – "

Meg stopped, remembering suddenly that she had not made up her mind. That she had told 'her John' to go away.

Aunt March was very angry. "Well, I wash my hands of the whole affair! You've lost more than you know, but I won't stop you. Just don't expect anything from me when you are married!" And, slamming the door in Meg's face, she drove off.

She seemed to take all the girl's courage with her, for Meg stood undecided whether to laugh or cry. Before she could make up her mind, Mr Brooke came back and put his arms around her.

"I couldn't help hearing, Meg," he said. "Thank you for defending me, and proving that you do care for me a little bit."

"I didn't know how much until she abused you," began Meg.

"And I needn't go away but may stay and be happy?"

"Yes, John," she whispered, and hid her face on Mr Brooke's waistcoat.

Fifteen minutes after Aunt March's departure, Jo came downstairs to the parlour, expecting to find that Meg had sent Mr Brooke away as planned. She was shocked to find him sitting on the sofa with Meg on his knee.

The lovers turned and saw her. Meg jumped up, looking both proud and shy, while 'that man', as Jo called him, actually laughed and kissed the astonished newcomer. "Sister Jo," he said, "congratulate us."

That was altogether too much! Jo vanished without a word and rushed upstairs. She startled the invalids by bursting into the room and saying, "Oh, *do* somebody go down quick! John Brooke is acting dreadfully and Meg likes it!"

Mr and Mrs March left the room at speed whilst Jo threw herself on the bed and told the news to Beth and Amy. But the little girls thought it most agreeable and interesting, and Jo got little sympathy from them. So she went up to her refuge in the garret.

Nobody ever knew what went on in the parlour that afternoon but a great deal of talking was done. The quiet Mr Brooke managed to explain his plans and persuade his friends to arrange everything just as he wanted it. Then he proudly took Meg into supper, both of them looking so happy that Jo hadn't the heart to be jealous or dismal. Amy was impressed by John's devotion and Meg's dignity. Beth beamed at them from a distance, and Mr and Mrs March looked very happy and satisfied.

"You can't say nothing pleasant ever happens now, can you, Meg?" said Amy.

"No, I'm sure I can't. How much has happened since I said that."

"It's been a year full of events, but it ends well after all," said Mrs March.

"I hope the next will end better," muttered Jo, who loved a few people very dearly and dreaded to lose their affection in any way.

"It will if my plans work out," said Mr Brooke, smiling at Meg as if everything was possible now.

"I've so much to learn before I shall be

ready, it seems a short time to me," said Meg.

"You have only to wait," said John, "*I am to do the work.*"

The front door banged and in came Laurie with a great bouquet of flowers for 'Mrs John Brooke'.

"I knew Brooke would have his way," he said. "He always does when he makes up his mind." He followed Jo into a corner of the parlour after the others had gone to greet Mr Laurence. "You don't look very festive. What's the matter?"

"You can't know how hard it is to give up Meg," said Jo.

"You don't give her up, you only go halves."

"It can never be the same again," said Jo.

"You've got me, anyhow. I'm not good for much, but I'll stand by you, Jo, all the days of my life, on my word I will!"

"I know you will," replied Jo, gratefully.

"Then don't be sad. I'll soon be through college and then we'll go abroad on some nice trip? Would that cheer you up?"

"I rather think it would, but there's no knowing what might happen in three years," said Jo, thoughtfully.

"That's true. Don't you wish you could look into the future and see where we'll all be then?"

"I don't think so," said Jo. "I might see something sad, and everyone looks so happy now."

Father and Mother sat happily together. Amy was drawing Meg and John, who were in a beautiful world of their own. Beth lay on the sofa talking to her old friend, Mr Laurence. Jo lounged in her favourite low seat with a serious, quiet look on her face. And Laurie, leaning on the back of her chair so that his chin was level with her curly hair, smiled and nodded at her in the long mirror that reflected them both.

And so the curtain falls on Meg, Jo, Beth and Amy.